"I never get involved with someone in my investigation." Neil spoke, with his finger on her cheek.

"Because you lose perspective?" Isobel asked.

"Because the guilty can seem innocent and the innocent can seem guilty. I always go by the book."

Neil's hand slid to her neck under her curly hair. The warmth of his skin felt so good…the touch of his fingers against her scalp so sensually right. When he tilted her head up and lowered his, she knew exactly what was going to happen.

He paused just an instant in case she wanted to back away. She knew she should. But she definitely didn't want to. Curiosity and need were much stronger than any admonition from her good sense that she was consorting with the enemy. Right now, Neil didn't feel like the enemy.

It wasn't her *enemy* whose arms she was in right now.

Dear Reader,

How does a woman go about finding a perfect mate?
I was fortunate. When I met my husband, we had an
immediate connection. Love at first sight? I don't know
about that. But we built on our connection until it
developed into a lifetime of love.

My heroine, Isobel, is thirty-five and has almost given up
the search for Mr. Right. She has family commitments
that most men wouldn't want to take on. However, when
she meets Neil, although the circumstances seem wrong,
the man seems right. Can she trust the feelings that
threaten to overtake her good sense...and most of all her
heart?

Book Five in THE WILDER FAMILY continuity series
was an absolute pleasure to write. I hope you enjoy
following Isobel and Neil's journey to happily-ever-after.

All my best,

Karen Rose Smith

HER MR. RIGHT?

KAREN ROSE SMITH

SPECIAL EDITION®

Published by Silhouette Books

America's Publisher of Contemporary Romance

Special thanks and acknowledgment to Karen Rose Smith
for her contribution to the WILDER FAMILY miniseries.

 SILHOUETTE BOOKS

ISBN-13: 978-0-373-24897-1
ISBN-10:   0-373-24897-0

HER MR. RIGHT?

Visit Silhouette Books at www.eHarlequin.com

Printed in U.S.A.

Books by Karen Rose Smith

KAREN ROSE SMITH

Award-winning author Karen Rose Smith has seen more than fifty romances published. Each book broadens her world and challenges her in a unique way.

Readers can e-mail Karen through her Web site at www.karenrosesmith.com or write to her at P.O. Box 1545, Hanover, PA 17331.

To the "gathering" group
from York Catholic High School's class of '67.
It's been wonderful reconnecting again.
Thanks for the friendship and good times.

Chapter One

"You work with elderly patients. Is that correct, Miss Suarez?"

Isobel felt as if she had been viewed under a high-powered microscope for the past five minutes. Neil Kane had the power to make her pulse race simply by passing her in the hall. It wasn't his status as an investigator for the Massachusetts Attorney General's Office that rattled her most. Rather it was her response to him as a man, with his sandy-brown hair graying at the temples, his strong jaw with its cleft at the center, his tall, trim and fit physique under a charcoal suit. He was attractive enough to turn the heads of most women.

She didn't want her head turned—especially not by a man who was trying to pin wrongdoing on hospital personnel. Who was attempting to discover fraud that could be the downfall of Walnut River General, or more insidiously, make a takeover by Northeastern HealthCare a probability instead of a possibility.

"Miss Suarez?" the investigator repeated, those gold-flecked brown eyes sending a tingle up her spine.

Isobel intended to select every word carefully. "I'm a social worker at this hospital, Mr. Kane. I tend to any patient whose case history finds its way to my desk."

They sat alone in his temporary office, a small conference room, with the door closed. A laptop was positioned in front of Kane and a legal pad sat beside it. From her seat around the corner of the table, she couldn't see what was on the screen of the laptop.

When the investigator leaned back in his chair and rubbed the back of his neck, his knee was very close to hers. She didn't move an inch.

"I think everyone who works at this hospital has taken a course on how to be evasive," he muttered.

She didn't comment. By age thirty-five, she'd learned when silence had more effect than a retort.

He blew out a breath and she suspected his day had been as long as hers. From what she'd heard, he'd been interviewing personnel in this room since seven-thirty this morning; he'd been here eleven hours straight.

"Miss Suarez. You told me you've worked here ten years." He leaned forward. "In that amount of time, what age group has occupied most of your attention?"

She could only pick up a hint of his cologne, something woodsy and very masculine. "I haven't kept track."

"Well, then, isn't it a good thing we have records and computer programs that *do* keep track." His voice had an edge to it that was part frustration, part anger.

Her own temper was precariously perched. "Why are you

asking me the question if you already have the answer? You know, Mr. Kane, if you try hard enough to catch a fish, you might catch the wrong fish."

His brows arched. "Meaning?"

Impatiently, she shoved her very curly, chin-length auburn hair behind her ear. "Meaning…everyone I work with at this hospital is dedicated to his or her profession. We're here to take care of patients, not in any way to take advantage of them. I don't know what you're specifically investigating—there are so many rumors floating around, I can't count them all—but whatever it is, maybe someone made a mistake. Maybe there was a computer error. Maybe there's no culprit or fraud or theft at all."

He studied her for a few very long moments. "What would you have our office do, Miss Suarez? Ignore the possibility of wrongdoing? Wouldn't the guilty love that!"

The buzz around the hospital was that Neil Kane was the enemy. Everyone from the chief of staff to the night security guard had banded together to treat him as if he were. They believed in each other and the work they did here. This hospital was about patient care. That could change drastically if North-eastern HealthCare took over. If a conglomerate ran Walnut River General, the hospital would consider financial well-being more important than helping the residents of Walnut River.

Frustrated herself by a long day made longer by Neil Kane's hard-edged questioning, she made a suggestion. "If you want to know what I do and who I help, shadow me. Shadow the doctors and nurses. See what we do in a day. Do that, and then ask your questions. At least then you'll be asking the *right* ones."

They sat in silence for a moment, both stunned by her outburst. Eager to avoid his gaze, Isobel looked down and dusted some imaginary lint from her skirt. She had worn a

lime-green suit today to celebrate spring and the beginning
of May. This was the time of year she liked best, and she
wanted to bring the idea of new beginnings inside. The
longish jacket hid the extra pounds she'd put on since she'd
moved back in with her dad. The chunky jasper beads she
wore around her neck carried shades of green and brown that
coordinated well with her tan silk shell. Neil Kane was
studying her necklace, studying her face, studying *her.*
Because she was being confrontational? Or because…

A man hadn't looked at her as an attractive woman in over
two years. She wasn't feeling attractive these days—not with
the extra fifteen pounds, not with her mass of curls needing
a trim, not with the circles under her eyes showing her fatigue.

Kane's voice lost its sharpness as he asked, "What *are* the
right questions?"

Was he serious? Did he really want to know? "The right
questions are the ones that matter. Do the professionals who
work here *care* about the patients? Do they punch in and punch
out, or do they work when they're needed? If they aren't
making salaries commensurate with pay at a larger hospital,
why do they stay? *Those* are the questions that would be a start."

"Tell me what *you* do in a day."

In spite of herself, Isobel noticed the stubble shadowing
Kane's jaw. She saw the tiny scar over his right brow. She
wondered if there was someone in his life who could ease the
creases around his eyes into laugh lines. Amongst all the
other rumors about him, she'd heard he'd once been a
homicide detective with the Boston P.D. Was that why he
seemed so… so…unyielding?

Leaning back a few inches, she took a calming breath. "I
check on patients I'm following to see how they fared overnight. My supervisor hands me the files on new admissions

that I can help. I'm always writing progress notes. I meet with families, confer with therapists and find placements in rehab facilities and nursing homes."

"Do you find yourself giving more time to some patients than others?"

He'd asked the question mildly as if it were just another in a long list. But for some reason, it put her on alert. "Some cases are more complicated."

"What do you do when there isn't family to consult?"

"I try to do what's best for the patient, of course."

"Of course."

The way he said it made her hackles rise, and her temper flipped to the ruffled side. "Are you accusing me of something?"

"Did it sound as if I was?"

"Talk about evasive," she murmured.

"*I'm* asking the questions, Miss Suarez. This isn't give and take. It's an investigation."

"A *preliminary* investigation. Doesn't that mean your office isn't even sure if there's anything to investigate?"

"You know the saying, where there's smoke…" He trailed off, letting her fill in the rest.

"There's another old saying—when a man looks for dirt, he'll miss the gold."

"Where did *that* come from?" He seemed mildly amused.

Isobel frowned. She felt as if he were laughing at her. The quote came from her dad. At sixty-eight, he spouted as much wisdom as he did complaints these days. "Do you have any more questions for me?" she asked curtly.

"Yes, I do. Tell me about Doctor Ella Wilder and J. D. Sumner."

Isobel considered how best to answer him then finally decided on "They're engaged to be married."

"How did they meet?"

"Is that another question you already know the answer to?"

"Humor me."

Everyone knew how Ella and J.D. had met. "Mr. Sumner had an accident. He slipped on the ice."

"Here at the hospital?"

"Yes, in the parking lot."

"And Dr. Wilder treated him."

"Yes."

"Do you know any more about it than that?"

Now Isobel was really puzzled. "I'm not sure what you mean."

"Did you know the nature of Mr. Sumner's injury?"

"I believe he had torn cartilage in his knee."

"Isn't arthroscopic surgery for torn cartilage usually done on an outpatient basis?"

Now she saw where this was going. "Mr. Sumner's case was a little different."

"Why is that?"

"In February he was a representative from Northeastern HealthCare."

"So he received extra special treatment?"

"All of our patients receive the same treatment, but J.D. was a stranger in town. He didn't know anyone, and he didn't have anybody to help him."

Kane leaned forward, his gaze piercing. "You were called in on the case?"

"No. There was no need for that."

"Because Dr. Wilder took a personal interest in him?" Kane asked mildly.

His tone didn't fool her for a minute. "What do you want to know?"

After a thoughtful pause, the investigator was blunt. "I want to know if he was charged for special treatment. He was kept longer than necessary."

Her defensive guard slipped into place once more. "I understand since you're from the Massachusetts Attorney General's Office that you have access to medical records as well as financial records. If that's true, you can verify why Mr. Sumner was kept."

"The medical records say he had a fever."

She shrugged. "And what does Mr. Sumner say?"

"He said he had a fever."

"Then why wouldn't you believe that?"

When Neil Kane wouldn't answer her question, she suspected why. Someone was feeding his office information—*false* information. There was a leak in the hospital and she guessed that someone in the administrative ranks was doing the damage. Someone had their own agenda to make the hospital look bad so Northeastern HealthCare could take over more easily.

Neil Kane seemed very close, though he hadn't moved and neither had she. "Patient records aside, can you tell me if Dr. Wilder transported Mr. Sumner at any time?"

"Why is *that* important?" she fenced, leaning back, putting more distance between them.

"I'm trying to understand what's fact and what's fiction, what are legitimate charges and what aren't."

The long day caught up to her. There was nothing of substance she could tell this man even if she wanted to. "My area is social work, Mr. Kane. Unless I'm following a case, I don't have contact or interaction with the other patients in the hospital."

"Oh, but I'm sure you hear plenty in your position. Besides

the fact that I understand that you and Dr. Wilder and Simone Garner are friends."

At that leap into personal territory, Isobel stood. "I understand you have an investigation to conduct. I don't like talking to you about my cases, but I will if I have to. But I *won't* discuss my personal relationships."

When he stood, too, she noticed he was a good six inches taller than she was and seemed to take up most of the breathable space in the room. That was her very overactive imagination telling her that, but nevertheless, oxygen seemed a little harder to come by. He wasn't menacing, but he *was* imposing.

"Are you going to stonewall me?" he asked in a low, determined tone.

"No. I'm just setting boundaries."

He frowned. "And what happens if I have to cross them?"

"I'll clam up and not talk to you at all."

As he studied her, he seemed to gauge her level of conviction. "There are consequences to obstructing an investigation."

"Do I need a lawyer?" she returned.

He blew out a long breath. "All right. You want to leave for now? Fine. Leave. But we're not done. I need answers and I intend to get them."

She could tell him he'd get those answers when hell froze over, but he *was* the one who held the power here. She was usually law-abiding and cooperative, but so much was at stake—the survival and reputation of Walnut River General.

Swallowing another retort, she picked up her purse, went to the door and opened it. Neil Kane didn't say another word, but she could feel his gaze on her back as she left the conference room. She suspected he wasn't the type of man who would give up easily. Still, round one went to her.

She wouldn't think about round two until it was staring her in the face...until Neil Kane was staring her in the face.

Then?

Then she'd deal with him again after a weekend of chores, sleep and gardening. Next week she was sure she wouldn't react to him so strongly. Next week she'd figure out how to be diplomatic. Diplomacy was usually her middle name. She'd just have to figure out why Neil Kane got under her skin...and make sure he didn't do it again.

Most of the houses in Isobel's childhood neighborhood had been built in the 1950s. She'd been five when her family had moved into the house on Sycamore Street, her sister Debbie seven, their brother Jacob three. She remembered the day they'd moved in to the modest brick two-story with its flowerpots on either side of the steps and the glassed-in back porch where she and her brother and sister played whenever the weather permitted. The neighbor on the left, Mrs. Bass, had brought them chocolate-chip cookies. The neighbor in the small ranch house on the right, Mr. Hannicut, had given her dad a hand unloading box after box from the truck someone had loaned him.

Isobel had never expected she'd be living back here again after being on her own since college.

The detached garage, which sat at the end of their lot in the backyard, only housed one car—her father's. Because of the shoulder surgery he'd had two weeks ago, he couldn't drive now. He hated that fact and so did Isobel because it was making him grumpy. Lots of things about his recuperation were making him grumpy.

She parked in front of the house knowing that he'd had his physical therapy appointment today. One of his senior center buddies had taken him.

Although May in Massachusetts brought warmer days, the nights could still be cold. Without a coat to protect her, she quickly opened the front door and called over the chatter of the television, "I'm home." She'd phoned him late this afternoon to see how his session had gone and to tell him she'd be late. He'd been monosyllabic, not a good indication that he'd be in a better mood tonight.

After a glance at Isobel, her father flipped off the TV. "It's about time."

He rubbed his hand over his shoulder as if it ached.

Isobel tried to put her fatigue aside and remind herself what her dad must be going through. "I'm sorry I'm so late. As I told you on the phone, I had a meeting."

"You need a job that doesn't run you ragged fifteen hours a day." John Suarez lowered the leg lift on his recliner, pushed himself to the edge of the seat, then used his right arm to lever himself up.

He was a stocky man who stood about five-eight. At sixty-eight, his black curly hair had receded but was still thick. His eyes were the same dark brown as Isobel's. She'd gotten her red-brown hair from her Irish mother.

The stab of memory urged Isobel's gaze to the photos of her family on the mantel above the fireplace.

Her father must have noticed. "She'd want you to slow down, go out and meet a nice young man and have some kids."

"As if wishing could make it so," Isobel murmured, then smiled at her father. "I like my work. You know that. And if Mom wants me to get married, she's just going to have to toss the right guy down here in front of my nose."

"I still don't understand why you broke up with Tim. He treated you nice. He owned his own business. Bicycle shops are really taking off these days. Sometimes I think you're just too picky."

Picky? She supposed that was one way of putting it. After her mother died, she'd moved back in with her father to ease his grief, to help with the chores, never intending to stay permanently in her childhood home. But her dad had begun having shoulder problems and was limited in what he could do for himself. Isobel had always liked cycling and she'd bought a new bike. The owner of a cycle shop, Tim, had asked her out and over the next year they'd gotten serious.

But Tim had never liked the fact that she lived with her dad. He'd insisted that if her father needed help, he should move into an assisted-living facility. Isobel had already lost one parent and she'd known how much the family home meant to her father. How could she suggest he leave when he still felt her mother's presence here? In the end, her father had been the reason she and Tim had broken up. Family was important to her. She'd never ignore or abandon them and that's what Tim had wanted her to do.

"Tim just wasn't right for me, Dad." She headed for the kitchen. "Give me ten minutes and I'll have that roast beef and mashed potatoes from last night warmed up."

"Cyrus and I finished the pie Mrs. Bass made, so there won't be any dessert," he called after her. "You really need to go to the store. We're out of ice cream and orange juice, too."

"I'll shop first thing in the morning, then I want to get out into the garden."

"If you plant flowers, they could still freeze overnight."

"I'll cover them." She just needed to work her hands into the earth, feel the sun on her head, and forget about everything going on at the hospital...especially Neil Kane.

For the next fifteen minutes, Isobel tried to put a meal

together. Unfortunately, she left the roast beef in the micro-
wave too long and the edges turned into leather. The mashed
potatoes weren't quite hot enough. The frozen broccoli was
perfect—except her dad didn't like broccoli. It had been the
only vegetable left in the freezer.

After he tried to cut a piece of meat with one hand, he
grumbled, "Spaghetti would be easier for me than this. Now
if I could saw it with both hands—"

Isobel felt tears burn in her eyes. "It was the best I could
do for tonight. Sorry." She really wanted to yell, "This isn't
the life I'd planned, either."

So many thoughts clicked through her head, memories of
the meals her mother had made that had always been perfect
in her dad's eyes, the family get-togethers around the table
every Sunday. But with her mom's death and her sister's
divorce, Sunday dinner had dwindled into now and then. Life
had changed whether they'd wanted it to or not. But her dad,
especially, didn't like the changes.

"Maybe we should keep some frozen dinners in the
freezer," he suggested helpfully.

Frozen dinners. Her mom would turn over in her grave.

"No frozen dinners. At least not the ones bought in the
store." She turned to face her dad. "What I should do is spend
all day Sunday cooking, make some casseroles that we could
freeze and you could just take one out and put in the oven
when I'm late."

"Did you have plans for Sunday?"

She didn't have *specific* plans for Sunday. She'd just been
looking forward to a day off, a day of rest, a day to catch up
with her sister and her niece and nephews, maybe go for a
walk along the river now that the weather was turning nicer.
Maybe go cycling again.

Instead of telling her dad about her hopes, she gave him a smile and answered, "No plans. I'll fill the freezer so we don't have to worry about meals for a couple of weeks."

He gave her a sly smile. "When you go to the store tomorrow, don't buy any more broccoli, okay?"

"No more broccoli," she agreed and started loading the dishwasher, exhausted, eager to go to bed so that she could get up early tomorrow morning to get grocery shopping out of the way and spend a couple of hours in the garden before she did laundry and the other household chores.

Isobel basked in the sun's warmth, digging her hands into the ground, making another hole for a Gerber daisy. It was the last of the six, a beautiful peachy-pink color she'd never seen before. She'd have to cover the flowers at night for a little while, but it would be worth the extra bother.

A shadow suddenly fell over her.

"Miss Suarez?"

She knew the voice without turning around to see who it belonged to, the voice she was so familiar with after just one meeting. She knew its timbre and depth and edge. It was Neil Kane's voice.

In some ways she wished she could just disappear into a hole in the ground. She was wearing a crop-sleeved T-shirt that came to her waist and old jeans that were grubby at the knees and too tight across her rear. She had no doubt she'd brushed peat moss across her cheek and her hands were covered with dirt.

Sitting back on her haunches, she closed her eyes, took a deep breath, then looked over her shoulder.

"Mr. Kane. To what do I owe this pleasure on my weekend off? It's supposed to be wild and fun and free." She couldn't help being a little bit sarcastic. He was making everyone's lives at the hospital miserable. Did he have to chase them down at their homes, too?

"If you don't want me here, I'll leave."

His sandy hair blew in the breeze. He was dressed in a tan-and-black striped Henley shirt and wore khakis. She spotted the sandy chest hair at the top button of his shirt. His three-quarter-length sleeves were snug enough that she noticed muscles underneath. His eyes were taking her in, not as if she were a grubby Little Orphan Annie, but as if she were Miss USA! Was there interest there? Couldn't be. She felt mesmerized for a moment, hot and cold and just sort of mushy inside.

Feeling defenseless on the ground with him looking down on her, she put one hand on the grass to lever herself to her feet.

He offered her his hand. "Let me help."

She would have snatched her hand away, but she probably would have tumbled back down to the ground in a very unladylike position.

His hand was large, his fingers enveloping and she felt like a tongue-tied naive teenager with a crush on a football player.

As soon as she was balanced on her feet, she pulled out of his grasp and saw his hand was now covered with dirt. "I'm so sorry." She caught a towel from her gardening basket and handed it to him.

He just wiped his hands together. "I'm fine. But I can see I'm interrupting you. Can you take a break?"

Actually she was finished but she didn't know if she wanted to tell him that. "You didn't answer my question. Why are you here?"

"I didn't like the way our meeting ended. You were upset and I didn't mean to upset you."

"I wasn't upset," she protested.

"Okay, not upset, angry. Everyone seems to be angry—if not downright hostile. We're not going to get anywhere like that. I know I'm asking pointed questions, but I have to get to the bottom of the rumors and complaints. If there is insurance fraud, don't you want to know? If you cooperate, wouldn't that be better for both of us?"

"I *am* cooperating."

The corners of his mouth definitely twitched up in a semblance of a smile. "If that was cooperation, I'd like to see resistance."

She felt her face getting hot, and not from the midday sun. "I feel as if you're trying to entrap me or the staff. As if you want to catch us in some little discrepancy—"

"I want the truth."

There was something about Neil Kane besides his sex appeal that got to her. Maybe it was the resolve in his eyes that told her he was sincere.

"I stopped by today to see if we could discuss everything more calmly over lunch."

"You're asking everyone you question to lunch?"

This time, a dark ruddiness crept into his cheeks. "No, but I don't get the feeling you're hiding anything. You seem to want to be careful so no one gets hurt. I understand that."

"In other words, you think I'm a pushover."

He laughed and it was such a masculine sound, her tummy seemed to tip over.

"That's exactly what I mean," he explained. "Although you try, you really don't watch every word you say. I get the feeling you're a straight shooter. So am I. I thought we could make some progress together."

Having lunch with the enemy wasn't a terrific idea. On the

other hand, Neil Kane wasn't going to go away until he was satisfied with the answers he got. No one would have to know she was talking to him and maybe, just maybe, she could do some convincing of her own.

"I found a place I like," he coaxed. "You can probably go like that if you want."

At first she thought he was laughing at her, but then she realized he wasn't. He was serious. Where was he going to take her—to a hot-dog stand?

"I'd like to change and wash the dirt off my face." She crouched down, gathered her gloves with the small gardening tools and plopped them into her basket.

Neil picked up a hoe and a rake lying beside the garden.

"You don't have to—" she began.

"Someone could trip over them." Now he was smiling at her.

She couldn't help but smile back. "You can just leave them on the porch."

"I can wait there."

"That's silly. No, come on in. My dad's watching TV. He might ignore you, but at least you can find a comfortable chair." She started up the stairs and he kept pace with her. As he propped the tools against the wall, she said, "Mr. Kane, about my dad—"

"Do you mind if we drop the formality? My name's Neil. We might feel less confrontational if we can at least call each other by our first names."

"Isobel's fine."

Their gazes caught…met…held. Until finally he asked, "What about your dad?"

Whenever she looked into Neil's eyes, she lost every coherent thought in her head. She made the effort to concentrate. "If he seems to ignore you or is grumpy, it's just him, not you. Please don't feel offended. He had surgery on his shoulder two weeks ago and he's not happy about it. He's limited as to what he can and can't do, and that frustrates him."

"It would frustrate anyone."

Neil seemed to understand and that was a relief.

As they crossed the foyer and went to the living room, her father didn't say a word, just kept his eyes glued to the TV where a biography of Dwight D. Eisenhower played.

"Dad, I want you to meet—"

"Not now. Shhhh."

She felt her cheeks flush and was about to apologize to Neil when he said, "My father told me he visited the Eisenhower farm when he was a boy."

Isobel's father swung his gaze to Neil. "No kidding. How'd that happen?"

"My grandparents apparently knew a friend of the family."

"You're from Pennsylvania?"

"No. I was born and raised in Massachusetts, but we took a couple of vacations there when I was a kid. I was interested in history so the Gettysburg Battlefield fascinated me. I enjoyed it almost as much as Hershey Park."

To Isobel's surprise, her father laughed, and then his gaze went to her, expecting introductions.

"Dad, this is Neil Kane. He's...he's..."

"An investigator for the state Attorney General's Office," Neil filled in.

"So *you're* the one who's been snooping around the hospital."

Instead of taking offense, Neil smiled. "Investigators always get a bad rap when they try to find the answers, don't they?"

Her father just grinned and pointed to the sofa, which sat at a right angle to his recliner. "Sit down and tell me about those trips to Pennsylvania. My parents moved up and down the East Coast. My dad had trouble finding work until they settled here."

Isobel was absolutely amazed her father had started talking to Neil like this. But then maybe he sensed another history buff.

Who would have thought?

As she ran up the stairs, she mentally pictured everything in her closet, trying to decide what to wear. Then she chastised herself. What she wore simply didn't matter. She wasn't going to try to impress a man who would be here today and gone tomorrow. She wasn't going to try to impress a man who thought she or other personnel at the hospital had committed some kind of crime.

No matter how easygoing Neil seemed today, or how gentlemanly, she had to be on her guard. Her future as well as the hospital's depended on it.

Chapter Two

"I never expected you to bring me here. Only the locals know about this place." Isobel's eyes were the deep, dark brown of rich espresso. Her smile was even a bit friendly.

As Neil sat with Isobel in his car parked on the gravel lot of The Crab Shack, his gut tightened. How long had it been since a woman gave him an adrenaline rush? How long had it been since he'd actually felt happy to be somewhere *with* someone?

Happiness had been a commodity he couldn't quite get a grip on ever since he'd lost his brother. Guilt had been a factor in that, a guilt he'd never been without.

But today, just looking at Isobel in her bright yellow T-shirt, her pin-striped yellow-and-blue slacks, he felt...good, damn good. And he shouldn't. He'd only stopped by her house and brought her here to get information. He normally didn't fraternize with witnesses in an investigation. He always proceeded by the book.

But stonewalled by most of the staff…

"Not everyone in Walnut River considers me an enemy," he joked, returning her smile. "I'm staying at the Walnut River Inn. Greta Sanford told me about this place. She said to ignore how it looked on the outside and ignore some of the customers *inside* and just concentrate on the food."

"You haven't tried it yet?"

"I haven't had the chance to explore."

He'd arrived a few days ago and since then he'd spent most of his time in that hospital conference room.

"I heard you stayed at the hospital most nights until after nine."

"Does someone post my whereabouts on a Web site so everyone can check what I'm doing?" He was half kidding, half serious.

She didn't get defensive but rather looked sympathetic. "Scuttlebutt in small towns travels at the speed of light. Especially if it can impact jobs and careers."

Neither of them was going to forget for a minute why he was here. If he thought he could make Isobel forget…

Why did he *want* to make her forget?

So she'd let her guard down.

Isobel unfastened her seat belt, opened her door and climbed out of the car.

The Crab Shack was just that—a shack located along the river about a mile out of town. There were about fifteen cars parked in the lot and a line of patrons extended out the door. The weathered gray wooden building looked as if it might collapse in a good storm.

"There's always a crowd on the weekends and evenings

are even worse," Isobel explained as they walked toward the restaurant. "There are a couple of tables by the river, though, that are empty. We could just order the food and sit there."

Neil had dated women who would never sit in the open air, let alone go near one of the weathered benches. Isobel didn't seem to mind the breeze riffling through her hair. Her curls always seemed to be dancing around her face. His fingers itched to see if they were as soft as they looked. He couldn't help but notice the way her knit top fit her breasts—not too tight, not too loose. A stab of desire reminded him again that he hadn't slept with a woman in months. But that was because not just any woman would do. Isobel, however…

"A picnic table's fine with me," he agreed, his hand going to the small of her back to guide her.

She glanced up at him. Their gazes held. She didn't shift away…just broke eye contact and walked to the end of the line.

Fifteen minutes later, they were seated across from each other on the gray-brown benches. Half their table was shaded by a tall maple. Neil had bought a basket of steamed crabs for them to share. Isobel had insisted that was plenty, and that was all she wanted. But he couldn't resist the cheese fries.

He set those on the table between them.

Isobel laid a stack of napkins next to the crabs. "This always gets messy."

He also didn't know many women who would agree to picking steamed crabs for lunch. "Have you lived here all your life?" His information-gathering on Isobel Suarez had to start somewhere.

"Yep. Except for college."

"You have a master's degree, right?"

Reaching for a crab, she expertly cracked it. "I went

straight through, summers too. I was lucky enough to earn a few scholarships to take some of burden off of Dad. The rest were loans, but I finished paying them off last year."

She sounded glad about that and he realized she was the responsible type. Unable to take his eyes from her, he watched as she picked apart a crab, slipped some of the meat from one of the claws, and popped it into her mouth. She licked her lips and he felt as if his pulse was going to run away. She seemed oblivious to the effect she was having on him.

"Did you go to college?" She colored a bit. "I mean I heard you were a detective with the Boston P.D. before you took a job with the state." She used her fingers to separate another succulent piece of crab.

"I went to college and earned a degree in criminal justice before I joined the police force."

"Why did you leave the Boston P.D.?"

He went silent for a moment, realizing just how uncomfortable it could be to answer questions that went too deep or zeroed in on what he wanted to talk about least. "I left because I was getting too cynical." He nodded to the dish of cheese fries. "Sure you don't want one? Mrs. Sanford said they're as good as everything else here."

Isobel took a good long look at them, then at the crab she was picking. Finally, she smiled. "Maybe just one." She picked up a fry with a layer of cheese, took a bite from the end...and savored it.

Neil shifted on the bench. Damn it, she was turning him on with no effort at all. He felt as if he'd been in a deep freeze and Isobel had suddenly pushed the warm current button.

She took another bite of the large fry and set it down on a napkin. "Why is it that everything that's pleasurable comes with a price tag?"

"Don't most things come with a price tag?"

Their table was cockeyed on the grass and they could both see the river. She looked toward it now. "You know that old line, *the best things in life are free?*"

He nodded as he studied her profile, her patrician nose, her high cheekbones, the few wisps of stray curls that brushed her cheek in front of her ear.

She went on. "I used to believe that was true. And maybe it *is* true when you're young. But as you get older, everything seems to have a price."

He wondered what she was thinking about that made her sad, but he knew exactly what she meant. His gaze followed hers to the water and he almost recoiled from it. The sight of the river brought memories that were painful. He never should have brought her here. He'd thought his mind would be on the investigation and he would dive into the usual background questions. He never imagined they'd get into a conversation like this.

"Are you involved with anyone?" he asked her, surprising himself.

Her big brown eyes found his and for a moment, he thought she wasn't going to answer him, or that maybe she would say it was none of his business, which it wasn't.

"No, I'm not involved with anyone. How about you?"

"Nope. No strings. No ties that bind. With my job, any kind of a relationship would be difficult. I travel. I have a home base but I'm rarely there."

"Boston?"

"Yeah. It's home, but not really. Do you have family?" he asked her. "I mean besides your dad."

"I have a sister, Debbie, who lives here in Walnut River. We were always close but since her divorce, I think we've gotten even closer. We have a younger brother, Jacob, who's an adventurer. I don't think he'll ever settle down. One month he's in Australia surfing, the next he's in South America helping to save the rain forest."

"Lives in the moment?" Neil asked.

"Totally."

"How long ago did you lose your mom?"

"Four years ago. I moved back in with Dad after she died because he just seemed so…lost. He was having more problems with his arthritis and had fallen down the basement steps one day when he'd done some laundry and hurt his shoulder. So it just seemed the right thing to do."

"You were on your own before that?"

"Oh, sure. Since college. I had my own apartment over on Concord."

"It must have been hard for you, moving back home." He absolutely couldn't imagine it, but then he didn't have the relationship with his parents that Isobel obviously had with her dad.

"It was really odd moving back home. I mean, I had been in and out of the house ever since college, dinners on Sundays, stopping in to see how my parents were. But when I moved back into my old room, it was like I recognized it but I'd outgrown it. I didn't want to change anything because Mom had decorated it for me and that was part of her. Yet it was a young girl's room and I wasn't young anymore."

"What did you do?" he asked, curious.

"I packed away my cabinet of dolls, put the cupboard in the basement and moved in my computer hutch and printer. I couldn't bear to part with the latch-hook rug my mom had made, but I hung a watercolor I had at my apartment and bought new curtains. A mixture of yesterday and today."

"So living with your dad isn't temporary?"

"I don't see how it can be. He needs me and I can't turn away from that."

Neil admired what Isobel was doing. How many thirty-somethings would give up their life to help out a parent? "You're fortunate to be close to your family."

"You're not?"

He'd left himself wide open for that one. "There's a lot of distance between us, especially between me and my father."

She broke apart another crab. "Is that your doing or his?"

If anyone else had asked him that question, he would have clammed up. But Isobel's lack of guile urged him to be forth-right, too. "I'm not sure anymore. At one time *he* put it there. Now we both keep it there."

"That's a shame. Because anything can happen at any time."

That was a truth he'd experienced as a teenager.

They ate in silence for the next little while, listening to the birds that had found their way to the maples, to the sound of the breeze rustling the laurels and the foliage along the river, to the crunch of gravel as cars came and went. Whenever their gazes met, he felt heat rise up to his skin. It was the kind of heat that told him taking Isobel to bed would be a plea-surable experience. But as Isobel had said, most things had a price. He had the feeling she wasn't the type of woman who lived in the moment. She was the type of woman who wanted a marriage like her parents had had and wouldn't even consider a one-night stand as an option. He wasn't consid-ering it, either. This was an investigation, not a vacation.

After she wiped her hands with a napkin, she smiled at him. "I'm full."

His pile of crab shells was much larger than hers, and he'd finished all but two of the fries.

"I really should get back," she said. "I have laundry to do and cleaning. I play catch-up on weekends."

His weekends were usually his own. The cleaning lady took care of his apartment and he sent out his laundry. Suddenly his life seemed much too easy compared to Isobel's.

They finished their iced tea and cleaned up the remnants of lunch. His hand brushed Isobel's as they reached for the same napkin. The electric charge he felt could light up the restaurant for a week.

She seemed as startled as he was. She blushed, shoved more crab shells onto a paper plate, then took it to a nearby trash can to dump it. Five minutes later, they were in his car headed for her father's house. He'd felt comfortable talking to her while they had lunch, but now, there was an awkwardness intertwined with their silence.

Before he'd even stopped the car, her hand was already on the door. She unfastened her seat belt. "Thanks so much for lunch."

He clasped her arm. "We didn't talk about the hospital."

"No, we didn't," she responded softly.

"I need to ask you more questions. Can you stop by my office after you're finished work on Monday?"

"I never know exactly when I'll be done."

"I know. It doesn't matter. When I'm not doing interviews, I'll be going through records."

She looked as if she wanted to protest again, to tell him no one at the hospital had done anything wrong, but then she gave a little sigh as if she knew any protest wouldn't do any good. "All right."

He felt as if he had to tell her this lunch hadn't been all about his investigation because he finally had to admit to himself it hadn't. "I enjoyed lunch with you, Isobel."

She didn't say anything, just stared at him.

He leaned in a little closer. The scent of her lotion or her perfume reminded him of honeysuckle. If he kissed her, would she taste as sweet as she smelled?

If he kissed her—

Mentally he swore and shifted away.

She opened the door and quickly climbed out.

Neil watched her walk up the path to the door. She didn't look back.

And neither did he. Something told him his attraction to Isobel Suarez could bring him nothing but trouble.

On Monday afternoon, Isobel stopped to say hello to the nurses at the desk on the surgical floor, then continued down the hall and rapped lightly on the door to Florence MacGregor's room. Her son, West, worked in the accounting department at the hospital.

As a high thready voice called for her to come in, Isobel pushed open the door. "How are you doing, Florence?"

The thin, petite lady almost looked swamped by white in the hospital bed. Her surgery had been recent—on Friday—and she was still pale with dark circles under her eyes. This was her second hip replacement. Her first had been about six months ago. She'd done well with that operation. But Isobel and the staff had noticed disorientation and memory problems even back then. Isobel had spoken to West about it, believing Florence should be evaluated for Alzheimer's. But as far as Isobel knew, West hadn't done that yet.

Isobel drew up a chair beside the bed and sat down. "How are you feeling today?"

"My hip hurts. West said you might be stopping in because I can't go home when I leave here." She sounded upset by that.

"No, I'm afraid you can't. Remember when you went to Southside Rehab after your last operation?"

Florence's eyes were troubled. "I remember exercising. I should be feeling better, don't you think? My surgery was so long ago."

Isobel realized reality for Florence slipped from now to the past, even to the future. "You just had your second surgery on Friday. That's only three days ago."

"Three days?" She looked down at her hip and leg and frowned. "Maybe I can't think straight because of the pain medicine they give me."

With Florence's first surgery, the staff had thought that might be the case. But a nurse had made notes on the intake sheet that Florence's memory seemed to fade in and out. Ella Wilder, her orthopaedic surgeon, had noted the same was true during her visits and checkups.

Isobel and West had spoken more than once about the responsibility of elderly parents and how they felt about it. They were of like minds. West lived with his mother to watch over her. However, Isobel was afraid Florence couldn't stay by herself even during the day for much longer even if she recovered completely from surgery. The staff at the rehabilitation hospital would talk about that with West, she was sure.

Isobel noticed the beautiful bouquet of flowers on the windowsill in a glass vase. "What pretty flowers."

"West sent them," Florence said proudly. "He knows I like pink and purple." There were pink carnations and purple mums, tall lilies, too.

"West came in just a little while ago to eat lunch with me. Have you had your lunch, dear?"

Isobel smiled at Florence's concern for her well-being. Her

lunch had been yogurt and salad in between patient visits. "Yes, I did have my lunch. Was yours good?"

"Oh, yes, very good. I had…I had…I know I had meat loaf yesterday. What did I have today?" Her blue eyes were confused and she looked frustrated. "I hate when I can't remember. I know West worries about that. He worries about other things too and I—" She stopped abruptly.

"What other things, Florence?"

Florence thought about Isobel's question, looked a little guilty, and then said, "Oh, I don't know. I can't remember that, either."

But this time, Isobel wasn't so sure that Florence didn't remember. What was she hesitating to say?

"Have you had any visitors besides West?"

"Lily. We've been friends for a long time."

"I'm glad she came. Maybe she can visit you while you're working on getting stronger, too."

"You mean at that place where I'm going to have physical therapy?"

"Yes. West and I will sit down with you tomorrow and show you the pictures from two different facilities. He's going to show you the one he thinks is best for you."

"He has pictures at home, too…in his desk."

After Florence's first surgery, she'd been transferred to Southside Rehab Facility. But her son hadn't been entirely satisfied with her care. So this time, he'd also gathered brochures on Pine Ridge Rehab.

Isobel checked her watch and saw that if she didn't leave now, she'd be late for a meeting in a conference room in the tower. Walnut River General had four floors but it also boasted a tower that had been a later addition, with conference rooms, boardrooms and guest suites for consulting physicians. The new chief of staff himself, Owen Randall, had asked her to attend this meeting so she didn't want to be late. The way this day was going, she might be here until nine o'clock tonight answering Neil's questions after she finished with her last case.

When she thought about Neil, her tummy fluttered and she remembered the way he'd leaned close to her in the car… when she'd thought he might even kiss her. But of course he wouldn't do that. Her own reaction to him had just colored her perception.

She had so many questions where he was concerned. Why had he changed careers? Why was there distance between him and his parents? Had he taken her to lunch to further his investigation…or because he liked her?

She might never know the answers.

"Why are you frowning, Isobel? Are you troubled by something?"

Florence's mind might be fading into the past, but she was still caring and helpful and kind. Isobel could see why West was determined to take care of his mother the best way he knew how.

"I'm sorry I can't spend more time with you, but I've been called to a meeting that starts in a few minutes and I don't want to be late." Standing, she pushed her chair back and then laid her hand on top of Florence's. "I'll stop in again tomorrow with West and we'll talk about rehab."

"Thank you for coming by. I wish West would meet a nice girl like you. Then he wouldn't worry about me so much."

Isobel just smiled and waved goodbye as she left Florence's room. From what Isobel knew of West MacGregor, he went for the intelligent, geeky types. He'd been dating someone in the records department but Isobel hadn't seen him with anyone lately. His hours were long ones, too, and with taking care of his mother…

Isobel knew all about those commitments.

Neil strode into the conference room knowing full well no one wanted him there. Owen Randall—with his silver hair and stocky build, his red tie perfectly knotted—came over as soon as he spotted him.

"I still don't understand why you'd want to sit in on a meeting to discuss the hospital's possible investment in a fitness center with a warm-water pool. No insurance would even be involved. This would be a center for recuperating patients who could follow a regimen of their own because they no longer need direct patient care."

Neil wasn't only at Walnut River General to investigate insurance fraud. Someone from the hospital was feeding his office information, and they didn't know who their informant was. Neil wanted to find that out as well as get to the bottom of the allegations. If he could put his finger on the informant, he might be able to figure out if this was a move by someone who wanted the takeover to take place quickly, or if it was someone who was genuinely worried about the way Walnut River General did its business. His interviews so far had turned up nothing.

Except a mighty potent interest in Isobel Suarez.

Trying to brush Isobel from his mind, and not entirely succeeding, he gave the chief of staff an answer. "I'm going to investigate every aspect of this hospital, right side up and inside out, any way I have to. You might as well get used to that." He was investigating in his get-it-done-by-the-book manner.

Randall didn't like his answer one bit and Neil could see that. "I want this investigation over and done with so we can fight this takeover with our armor intact."

"Then tell everyone to cooperate with me," Neil suggested.

"I have," Randall returned indignantly. "And so has J. D. Sumner."

"Where *is* the hospital administrator today?"

"He had a meeting in Pittsfield. There's a trauma center there and if he likes what he sees, we'll model ours after theirs."

Neil had to admit the people he'd talked to here seemed like good people, but he knew from experience the real story was often hidden beneath the surface.

Although Peter Wilder and his fiancée, Bethany Halloway, gave him a nod, none of the other board members acknowledged his presence. He was used to being treated as an outsider and an enemy. But sometimes he wondered what it would be like to be an *insider.*

Owen had just introduced the board member who was going to run the meeting when Isobel opened the door and came hurrying in.

"Sorry I'm late," she murmured, slipping into the empty seat across from Neil. When she saw him, she looked surprised, but then she gave him a little smile.

He didn't know why that smile was so welcome. Why it warmed some place cold inside of him. Or why Isobel suddenly seemed to be the only other person in the room.

Paul Monroe, a board member who owned his own contracting firm, stood at the head of the table holding a sheaf of papers in his hand. He passed a handout to each person at the table. "This is the result of our feasibility study. There's no question that a fitness center subsidized by clients as well as the hospital would be a success in Walnut River. With the number of residents in the general community who we believe would use this facility, we could easily break even or turn over a small profit."

One of the female board members asked, "And how would this be different from a health club?"

"Isobel, would you like to answer that?" Monroe asked, then went on to explain to the board, "Isobel has contacts with medical personnel, rehab facilities and doctors' offices that she deals with. She left questionnaires in all those offices and doctors had their patients fill them out."

Isobel looked a bit flustered, but stood and smiled at the group. "Anyone who would use this fitness center would need a prescription from his or her primary physician, which would indicate a medical condition. On the questionnaires many patients commented that they hate the regimen, the cost and the insurance hassles with physical therapy. With this center, they would pay a monthly fee, like a commercial gym."

"Would needing to lose weight apply?" asked a male board member who was about twenty pounds overweight. .

"It would," Isobel answered, then continued, "As long as the patient is being monitored by his doctor."

"Why a warm-water pool?" the man next to Neil asked. "Who would want to swim laps in warm water?"

Isobel didn't seem ruffled at all as she answered calmly, "If a patient can swim laps, he probably wouldn't need the use of *this* pool. But anyone with arthritis, fibromyalgia, sports injuries, even continued rehabilitation after a stroke would benefit from a warm-water pool." She gestured to a pretty young woman. "Melanie, do you want to explain the benefits?"

Melanie Miller introduced herself as a physical therapist and Neil listened with half an ear. His attention was still on Isobel—her sparkling brown eyes, the professional way she fielded questions, the energy she brought to a room. She was wearing a conservative royal-blue suit, yet the silky top under her jacket was feminine. She wore a silver chain around her neck with one dangling pearl. He was too far away to catch the scent of perfume but he remembered the honeysuckle sweetness he'd inhaled on Saturday.

While Melanie answered questions, Isobel took her seat again, and her gaze met his, once, twice, three times. After a moment or two, maybe feeling the same connection he did, she looked down at her notes, at another board member, anywhere but at him.

Was this attraction one-sided?

Damn it, there shouldn't be any attraction. Isobel was under investigation just like everyone else.

The discussion continued for about a half hour and then, as at most meetings like this, nothing was decided except that the hospital would have to consult with a fund-raising expert.

Randall took the floor once more. "I'll send a memo to all of you as to the time and place of our next meeting. We'll be sure J.D. is present so he can give us his thoughts, as well as any other staff member who is interested. Thank you all for your time. Your attendance is appreciated."

Neil took note of which board members spoke to other board members, and of how Melanie conversed animatedly with Isobel. Most important, he noticed who seemed to be the most hostile, who ignored him, and who didn't seem to care that he was there. Nonchalantly he stood and walked out into the hall, catching bits and pieces of conversations.

When Isobel emerged, she saw him propped near a window, merely observing. The hallway was empty for the moment as she approached him. "I was surprised to see you at the meeting."

"I'm poking my nose into everybody's business. That should ruffle feathers and shake loose some information."

Another board member exited the conference room, spied Neil, and headed in the opposite direction.

"I'm sorry everyone's being so cool to you."

He shrugged. "It goes with the territory. I have a thick hide. I can take it."

"I imagine you can, but it's not a pleasant way to work."

Much of his work wasn't pleasant, but it *was* challenging. The only thing he didn't like particularly was all the traveling. That traveling had broken up his marriage. At least that's what he and Sonya had blamed it on. Now he wasn't so sure. He'd done a lot of soul-searching since his divorce and a contributing factor was definitely his penchant for keeping his own counsel, for not letting anyone get too close, including his ex-wife. During the marriage he hadn't realized he was closing Sonya out. But afterward…afterward he'd understood he'd closed people out since his brother had died when Neil was in high school. He had good reasons for wanting to protect himself, for not confiding in anyone, for dodging his feelings. Preventing self-disclosure had become a habit, a habit he'd taken with him into his marriage.

Skipping over Isobel's comment, he said, "You seem to be the go-to person for Randall on this project."

"Peter Wilder suggested Mr. Randall include me in the discussion."

"The Dr. Wilder who was chief of staff after his father died?"

"That was only temporary. Peter's not a paper-pusher. He likes treating patients. But yes, he's the one."

"And Peter Wilder is Ella Wilder's brother, correct?"

"Yes."

"And also Dr. David Wilder's brother—the physician who was called in to help with the little girl who needed plastic surgery."

"Yes. Their father was well-loved as chief of staff. He was an extraordinary man. His children are as dedicated as he was. Except…"

"Except?" Neil prompted.

"Anna Wilder. She's Peter, Ella and David's adopted sister. Ironically, she happens to work for Northeastern Health-Care."

Neil looked shocked. "Now *that* I hadn't heard."

Isobel looked troubled. "I probably shouldn't have said anything."

"I'm glad you did. Isobel, I need to know the ins and outs of what's going on here right now. That's the only way I'll get to the truth."

Two more board members and Owen Randall emerged from the conference room. All three exchanged looks when they saw Neil and Isobel together talking.

Isobel's cheeks reddened and she murmured, "I have to get back to work."

"You'll stop at my office before you go home?"

"Yes." Without a "goodbye," "see you later" or "it was nice talking to you," she hurried to the elevator.

Randall was staring after Isobel thoughtfully.

Neil would give her a couple of minutes to get away from him and then he'd take the elevator to his office. Better yet, maybe he'd just take the stairs.

He knew why Isobel had hurried away. She was a member of this hospital community. She had respect here and lots of friends. She didn't want to be seen consorting with the enemy.

Neil hated the idea of being Isobel's enemy. His job had never interfered with a personal relationship with a woman before.

But there was *no* personal relationship here. He was just going to do his job and return to Boston.

So why had Isobel's rushing away gotten to him?

Chapter Three

Neil definitely had a height advantage.

When Isobel entered his office and he stood, she felt small. His size could be intimidating if he wanted it to be.

He'd been working at the table again, printouts spread all over it. He motioned to the extra chair. "Did you get a breather or did you come straight from working?"

"No breather. I had a consultation with one of the doctors about a patient."

She lowered her briefcase and purse to the floor and sank into the chair. She knew she had to be alert and on guard in this setting with Neil. Maybe in all settings with Neil. She didn't know if he separated the personal from the professional and couldn't take the chance that he didn't. She'd been a little too open during their lunch, not that she'd revealed anything she shouldn't have. She wasn't a guarded person by nature.

But she didn't know what Neil might use against her, against other personnel, against the hospital.

He looked at her as if sensing her apprehension. "Isobel, I'm not going to attack you," Neil said quietly.

"Of course, you aren't. I mean, I didn't think you would."

"As soon as you sat in that chair, your shoulders squared, your chin came up and you looked at me as if I were the enemy. I'm not."

But his saying it didn't make it so.

He sighed. "Let's start with something easy."

She didn't comment.

"You mentioned Anna Wilder works for Northeastern HealthCare. Has that caused a rift in the Wilder family?"

"You'd have to ask the Wilders." Peter had come to her last month in confidence to talk over the situation. She was afraid she hadn't been much help. Peter, David and Ella were on one side and Anna on the other. Every conversation they had seemed to push them further apart.

"I *will* talk to the Wilders," Neil assured her. "But I just wondered if Peter, David and Ella are really all on the same side. They might portray a united front, but could one of them want to help their sister? Could one of them be feeding information to my office?"

This wasn't the kind of questioning Isobel had expected. She'd thought he'd be asking about dollars and cents and patient charges.

Considering his question, she answered honestly, "I think it's highly unlikely. Peter, Ella and David are very straightforward in what they believe and they've all been vocal in how they feel about the takeover."

"But it's possible one of them could be sympathetic to Anna?"

She thought about her strong relationship with her sister, Debbie, and her brother, Jacob, and remembered what Ella had told her about the bonds between her and her adopted sister, Anna, when they were small. "I suppose it's possible."

Neil looked thoughtful and glanced down at the legal pad where Isobel could see a list of scratchings. She couldn't make out most of the writing, but her name was clearly printed at the top.

"I understand no one objected when Peter Wilder temporarily took over the position of chief of staff." Neil was fishing again. "Was anyone surprised when Peter didn't keep the position? Were *you* surprised?"

"Actually, I wasn't sure what Peter would do. I mean, I knew patient care was important to him. He's the epitome of a caring doctor. Yet maintaining his father's legacy was important, too. So I imagine the decision he made wasn't easy. In the end, I guess he did what he knew would make himself happy, and that was taking care of patients. Why are you so interested in the Wilders?"

"Because they're involved in everything—the running of the hospital, interaction with patients, the board, as well as their connection to the takeover. I imagine a family like that is not only respected but can make enemies just by being who they are. If, as you believe, the allegations my office is investigating have no merit, I have to look for other reasons why anyone would want me to give them credence."

Could someone be feeding false information to the state Attorney General's Office because he or she had a grudge against the Wilders? That was possible, Isobel surmised.

"Tell me about David Wilder. Why did he return to Walnut River?"

Isobel leaned forward and accused, "That's another one of those questions you already know the answer to."

A small smile played across Neil's lips and she couldn't seem to move her gaze from them.

"Indulge me," Neil suggested once again.

"David's a renowned plastic surgeon. He came back to Walnut River to help a little girl who needed reconstructive work done."

"Not because of the takeover attempt?"

"I don't think so. But I don't know for sure. He probably knew about it but he was here to help Courtney's little girl."

"Courtney Albright who works in the gift shop?"

"Yes."

"But she and David Wilder are now engaged."

"Yes."

"Do you know if his airfare was charged to a hospital account?"

"I don't know. But if it was, there wouldn't be anything wrong with that, would there? After all, if he was asked to come as a consultant—"

The beeping of Isobel's cell phone in her purse interrupted them. "I need to check that," she said. "It might be my father. With him at home alone—"

"Go ahead." Neil didn't look impatient or even annoyed, and that surprised her. Didn't he want to get this questioning over and done with as much as she did?

She opened her phone, saw her sister's number on the screen and became alarmed. What if something *had* happened to their dad?

"Debbie, what's wrong? Is Dad okay?"

"Sorry to scare you, Iz. Dad's okay as far as I know, but I need your help."

"What's wrong?"

"Chad had an away game and his bus broke down on the way home."

Isobel's nephew Chad was sixteen and hoping to get a baseball scholarship to college. Since his mom and dad had divorced two years ago, he'd become more quiet, more withdrawn. He obviously missed his father who had moved to the Midwest to take a better job and start a new life. Chad was a big help with his younger brother and sister but sometimes Isobel thought Debbie's older son felt he had to take his dad's place, and that could be a burden for a sixteen-year-old.

"What do you need?"

"Can you come over and watch Meg and Johnny while I go get Chad? I wouldn't lay this on you but I can't find anybody else."

Isobel's niece was six and her nephew was four. "I can come over but I'm in a meeting right now and I'll have to stop and pick up Dad first. He's been alone so much lately, I hate to have him spend the evening at the house by himself."

"Isobel." Neil's voice cut into her conversation with her sister.

"Hold on a minute, Debbie."

"What's going on?" Neil asked.

Succinctly she told him.

"I have a few more questions for you but they aren't as important as helping your sister. Why don't I go pick up your father and bring him to wherever you need him to be?"

Isobel was stunned. "Are you serious? Why would you want to help?"

"Maybe because I'm a stranger in town and I have nothing else to do."

Sure, Neil might just want to fill his time, but she saw a

kindness in him she hadn't seen in a man for a long while. Should she accept his offer? What would he expect in return?

"Isobel?" her sister called to her from the phone.

"What?"

"The boys are standing by the side of the road and I really want to get there as soon as I can. Can you cut your meeting short?"

Isobel's gaze met Neil's. She wasn't sure what she saw there. Curiosity? Interest? Desire? Was her imagination tricking her into thinking this man might be interested in her? She didn't even want his interest, did she?

Yet being closed in this office with him, inhaling the musky scent of his cologne, appreciating the baritone of his voice as well as his desire to get to the truth, she had to admit she did want to get to know him better, in spite of the consequences or the risk.

"You're sure you want to do this?" she asked him.

He nodded. "I'm sure. I can have all this packed up in three minutes. Tell your sister you'll be there as soon as you can."

As Isobel did just that, she wondered if she was making a terrible mistake.

Neil gave Isobel's sister's kitchen a quick study as he pushed open the screen door for John Suarez and juggled two pizza boxes.

A little girl came running to meet the older man, her dark-brown pigtails flying. She looked to be about the age of a first-grader.

"Grandpa, Grandpa. Will you play dominoes with us? Aunt Iz said I should ask."

Aunt Iz? Neil had to smile as he followed her father

inside the cheery kitchen with its purple-pansy and yellow-gingham theme.

A little boy in jeans and a Spider-Man T-shirt added, "Will you play with us? Will you play with us?" to his sister's question.

Neil leaned close to Isobel. "Aunt Iz?"

"Only my family uses that nickname, so don't get any ideas."

He inhaled the honeysuckle scent surrounding her and right away noticed her change of clothes to jeans and a powder-blue T-shirt with a sleeping cat on the front. Printed under the white feline, the print said Don't wake me unless there's an emergency.

When she spied him reading her T-shirt, she explained, "I always keep a duffel bag in my car with a change. It comes in handy." Monitoring what her niece and nephew were doing, she warned gently, "Don't pull on Grandpa's arm."

"I smell pizza," the little boy said and came over to stand in front of Neil. "Who are you?"

Neil hadn't been around children much, but he appreciated forthrightness in anyone. He crouched down to the little boy's level, pizza boxes and all. "I'm Neil Kane. I'm working at the hospital right now with your aunt, and I brought supper."

The supper part of the explanation intrigued Isobel's nephew most. "Mom only lets us order pizza one time a week." He held up his index finger and stared at the boxes with longing. "I like pepperoni. Did you bring pepperoni?"

Neil laughed and stood. "Yes, I did. Your grandfather said that was your favorite."

"Can we eat now?" the boy pushed.

Isobel ruffled her nephew's hair. "Why don't you tell Mr. Kane your name first."

"My name is Johnny, after Grandpa." He pointed to his sister. "And her name is Meg. *Now* can we eat?"

"You get the napkins. I'll get the silverware. Neil, can you set those on the table?"

Isobel was a manager, no doubt about that.

After they were all seated at the table and Isobel's father had rolled his pizza so he could eat it one-handed, she asked him, "How did physical therapy go today?"

"They're trying to turn me into a muscle man. I just want to be able to use my arm again."

"You're doing exercises with repetitions now?" she asked.

"Yeah." Isobel's dad studied his grandchildren happily munching their pizza and then turned to Isobel and Neil. "This was a good idea, Iz."

"It was Neil's," she admitted, looking up at him, a slight flush on her cheeks.

Was she feeling the heat, too? Had she been fantasizing about a kiss between them? Maybe more?

As if maybe, just maybe, the same thoughts were running through her mind, she broke eye contact and concentrated on cutting her pizza into little pieces.

"Do you always eat it like that?" Neil asked her.

"I'm only having one piece and it will stretch it out."

"My daughter believes she needs to lose weight," John explained. "What do *you* think, Neil?"

"Dad!" Isobel protested, sounding horrified he'd bring up the subject at the table.

"I think Isobel's perfect the way she is," Neil said, meaning it.

John Suarez cocked his head and with a twinkle in his eye, asked, "How long are you going to be in Walnut River?"

"As long as it takes to finish my investigation. Probably about three weeks."

"That's a shame. Do you think you'll ever consider settling down some day?"

"Dad!" Isobel protested again.

"I don't know, Mr. Suarez. I've been doing this job for a long time. Traveling is a big part of it."

"Life changes. Needs change," Isobel's dad advised sagely. "Have you ever been serious about someone? Just wanted to be where they were?"

This time when Neil glanced at Isobel, she didn't protest, she just looked mortified. She murmured, "Dad doesn't respect boundaries."

"Boundaries, schmoundaries," her dad muttered. "Maybe it's a question you've wanted to ask him and didn't have the guts."

Isobel looked as if she wanted to throw her napkin at her father. But instead, she put it in her lap, her lips tight together. She was probably biting her tongue.

Meg and Johnny seemed oblivious to the conversation as they stole pieces of pepperoni from each other's slices of pizza.

Neil knew he could joke off the question. However, if Isobel had wanted to ask it and was too shy to, he might as well give her the answer. "I was married once, but traveling was hard on the relationship."

"That's why you split?" John pressed.

"Not entirely. But it *was* a major stumbling block. My ex-wife and I were naive to think we would stay close when we were miles apart most of the week."

Isobel's father finished another roll of pizza and wiped his mouth with his napkin. "Naive… Or maybe the two of you didn't want to *be* close."

"All right, Dad." Isobel stood. "Meg, Johnny, if you're

finished playing with each other's pizza, why don't you wash up? We could set out the dominoes on the coffee table and we'll all play a game." She looked at Neil. "Unless you need to leave."

He was still trying to digest the fact that Isobel's father had gotten to the bottom of the problem with his marriage with such clarity. "No, I don't have to leave yet." Then he turned to John. "How long were you married?"

"When Brenna died, we'd been married forty-one years. We weren't apart even one night, not even when she had our babies. I remember they tried to keep me out of the labor room with Isobel, but I wouldn't let them. I told them Brenna was my wife and I was staying. When she got sick—" He shook his head as if the memories hurt him deeply to remember. "I stayed in that hospital room every night. My doctor got me special permission because he understood. When you love someone, you walk through hell for them. Getting a crick in my neck sleeping on one of those hospital chairs was nothing compared to the comfort of holding her hand." He sighed. "But I don't think young people understand that kind of love anymore."

"You and Mom had something special. Jacob, Deb and I knew that," Isobel remarked in a quiet voice.

"Then why can't the three of you find it?" her father demanded. "Jacob runs off here and there as if he's searching for something and he doesn't even know what it is. Debbie…Debbie divorced her husband after his affair. They didn't even try to work it out."

"Dad, you don't know—"

"What else Ron did to her," he finished as if he'd heard it all before. "Maybe I don't. She won't talk about it with me. And then there's *you*. You work, work, work. I think that's the reason you and Tim broke up, though you'll never tell me the truth about *that,* either."

The tension and strain of having dirty laundry shaken out in front of Neil made Isobel's body taut. Beside her, Neil could feel it. Then she took a very big breath, seemed to somehow relax her muscles, and said to her father without any anger at all, "I know you must have a good reason for wanting to talk about all this in front of Neil, but it's making me uncomfortable and it's probably making him uncomfortable, too. Can we just relax the rest of the night? Play a little dominoes and talk about anything that isn't serious?"

John waved at his daughter. "That's her assertive, social-worker's side coming out. I hate feeling like I'm being handled," he grumbled. Then he smiled at his middle child. "All right, I'll keep my mouth shut."

"I don't want you to keep your mouth shut, Dad, but I would imagine that you and Neil can find a hundred topics more fascinating, especially since you both watch the History Channel."

Neil couldn't help but chuckle. When he looked over at John, the older man gave him a wink. "My daughter does have a point."

Isobel wasn't simply a caring daughter. She was an intelligent and beautiful woman who could turn him on with just the hint of a smile.

But this attraction could go nowhere. When he left, he'd go back to his life and she'd stay in hers.

End of story.

An hour later, when Isobel's sister and her older son came home, Neil was making a quarter disappear for Johnny. The little boy had gotten tired of dominoes.

After Chad and Neil were introduced, Neil asked him, "So do the Sox have a chance at the pennant this year?"

Chad had reddish-brown hair like Isobel and the same brown eyes. He gave Neil a crooked smile. "As good a chance as last year. You follow baseball?"

"Since I was eight."

"You play sports in school?" Chad asked.

"Basketball."

"What did you play?"

"Center," Neil answered. "How about you?"

"Point guard."

"So you're busy all year."

"Mom wants to see me busy so I stay out of trouble."

His mother didn't deny it. Debbie was taller and thinner than Isobel, but had the same dark-brown eyes. Her hair wasn't as curly and it was more brown than red but the resemblance was there.

Chad spotted the pizza box. "Was there any left over?"

Neil nodded. "It's in the refrigerator."

Johnny came running over and tugged on his brother's arm. "He can make a quarter disappear."

Chad gave his brother's shoulder a little bump. "You can make quarters disappear when you go to the candy machine in the mall."

"Not like that," Johnny protested. "Show him," he demanded.

Neil suddenly realized how much he was enjoying the evening, how long it had been since he'd spent time with a real family. During investigations he usually felt isolated. Each meeting was a confrontation and he spent every night by himself. Looking around at this close family, he realized how tired he was of the whole routine. His gaze fell on Isobel. She was sitting on the sofa with Meg and tying her niece's shoe. She held the little foot in her hand so gently, smiled so tenderly at Meg, that Neil actually felt his heart lurch.

What was happening to him?

Whatever it was, it unsettled him. Didn't he have the life he wanted? Hadn't he decided an intimate relationship only brought pain and disappointment?

Yet whenever he looked at Isobel, he had a yearning inside that told him that maybe the life he'd been leading wasn't fulfilling enough.

Disconcerted by his thoughts, his life, an investigation that seemed to be going nowhere fast, he checked his watch. "I'd better be going. I still have some work I want to do tonight."

"Thanks for bringing me over here," John said, "and for the pizza. Don't be a stranger. I could use a little company now and then."

"I'll keep that in mind," Neil told the older man.

Isobel crossed to him and walked him to the door. He'd discarded his suit coat long ago, tugged down his tie, rolled up his shirtsleeves. She was taking him in, just as he was taking her in. The chatter of her family behind them in the kitchen reminded him they weren't alone.

"You have a nice family."

"They liked you. I could tell."

"That's because I know how to make quarters disappear."

Isobel laughed. "I think they like you for more than magic tricks."

"You're fortunate to be able to be around people who care about you."

"Sometimes they annoy me," she admitted with a sly grin. "But most of the time I know they love me. I'm sorry you don't have that kind of support."

Neil shrugged. "I've gotten used to it. I'm basically a loner so I don't miss it."

Isobel tilted her head and studied him. "I think you've convinced yourself of that, but I don't know if it's true."

He wasn't going to delve into his personal history or give her a glimpse into his family's dynamics. They hardly knew each other. Yet in some ways he felt Isobel knew him better than most people did.

He reached out and brushed a few curls away from her cheek, his fingers burning from the contact. Touching Isobel was such a temptation!

He caught the spark of desire in her eyes and fell back on the investigation that was always between them. "I still have some questions for you, but my next few days are booked solid. I'll call your office at the end of the week and we can set up another appointment."

He found himself not wanting to leave Isobel and that was absolutely crazy. Also, out of the question. He always left. That's how he lived his life.

Alone.

As soon as Neil drove away, Isobel touched her cheek where his fingers had grazed her skin. She could still feel the tingling heat of his touch.

Debbie opened the screen door and stepped outside. "Your taste in men has improved. This one is not only good-looking, but he seems to like family."

"My taste in men had nothing to do with Neil being here. We were having a meeting and he offered to help out."

"He wouldn't have offered if he wasn't interested."

"In me?" Isobel laughed. "I doubt that. We're on opposite sides of an investigation."

"He looked at you as if he's interested. I was watching."

She and Debbie didn't have many secrets. "The truth is—

I don't know if I can trust him. He might just want to get more information out of me."

"You have good radar, Izzy. What's it telling you?"

"My radar usually isn't compromised by an—"

"Attraction?" Debbie smiled. "You like him."

"Even if I did, that doesn't matter. He'll be leaving in a few weeks. You know I'm not the type to live in the moment."

"Maybe living in the moment wouldn't be such a bad idea. It might even be fun. Think about it, Iz…having fun. If you're given the chance, maybe you should try it."

Isobel didn't want to have fun now and exchange that for heartache later.

But when she thought of Neil's touch and the exciting golden light in his eyes, she was afraid he could convince her otherwise.

Chapter Four

As West MacGregor hurried down the hall to his mother's room on Tuesday afternoon, one of the nurses waved to him. Tami had a nice smile and was always friendly. With her divorce final now, maybe he should ask her out. He straightened the knot on his tie. Unlike many men, he felt comfortable in a suit and tie. His professional attire defined him, gave him purpose and his place in the world. As an accountant at Walnut River General, his services were necessary to the running of the hospital. Tami was one of the people here who respected his position.

His position.

He'd led his life on the straight and narrow—his mother had taught him well. His father had split before he'd entered first grade. His mom's secretarial skills and her promotion to executive secretary to the vice president of an engineering firm had supported them well enough for her to buy a small house and even give West money toward college. He owed her. He owed her for raising him right. He owed her for making sure he had a place to go after school when she had to work. He owed her for just being there whether it was for his school concert or parents' day at college. She'd been a wonderful mother, giving him everything she possibly could, and he wasn't going to let her down now when she needed him most.

That's why being a corporate spy didn't bother him as much as it should.

West glanced down at the brochures for rehab facilities in his hand, then thought about the "other" pamphlet in his desk at home, along with the information packet about Fair Meadows. Fair Meadows had everything his mother would need when she could no longer stay alone. They could be at that point in four to six months, maybe a year if they were lucky.

After she'd recuperated from her first hip operation, he'd taken her to Boston for an evaluation. He'd wanted the best doctors in the Alzheimer's field looking after her. He also hadn't wanted hospital scuttlebutt talking about it, her or them. Driving her to Boston had enabled him to do what he was doing now without throwing any suspicion on himself.

He wasn't doing anything illegal, exactly. He was just feeding information that was a bit skewed to the Massachusetts Attorney General's Office, as a favor for Northeastern HealthCare. The conglomerate was funding his mother's care until she needed to be admitted to Fair Meadows. Not only was he receiving a lump sum for whatever his mother might need, but the head honcho at Northeastern HealthCare had promised to find a room for her at Fair Meadows when she needed it. The facility's waiting list was a mile long.

West really had no choice but to help NHC. His salary wasn't enough to cover long-term care, and he would not let his mother become a ward of the state in some second-rate nursing home where she'd be miserable and he'd worry daily about her care. She deserved more than that, and he was going to see that she got it.

As West approached his mother's room, he heard voices coming from inside and recognized Isobel Suarez's. He liked Isobel—he really did. They had the same consideration for family. But he'd caught her talking to Neil Kane more than once and that worried him. Not because they were talking, but because they'd looked *friendly* while they were talking. If everyone treated Kane like the enemy, it would take him longer to get to the bottom of the information West had fed his office. He'd find most of the allegations groundless, though a few could be considered in the gray area. But the longer Kane's investigation took, the more headway Northeastern HealthCare could make in staging their takeover.

West strode into his mother's room determinedly cheerful as he always tried to be when he was with her.

She spotted him and her blue eyes danced a little, the way they used to. "Here's West now. Maybe he remembers that trip I took to Puerto Rico with Lily and Mary."

The trip to Puerto Rico. West had heard about that often but it had taken place before he was born.

Instead of walking down that road of conversation, he nodded to Isobel, smiled and suggested, "How about considering taking a trip when you're finished with rehab? You always wanted to visit Las Vegas. We can play the slots and go to shows."

"Could we really do that?"

"I have vacation time and it would be a great incentive for you to get better fast."

Isobel was taking in their conversation. "So you like to play the slot machines?" she teased his mother.

"West took me to Atlantic City a few times. I won a two-hundred-dollar jackpot once."

That had been about five years ago. Sometimes his mother's memory was more detailed than his. He'd once heard that if there was a lot of feeling attached to memories, they lasted longer. Holding up the brochures, he went to the bed and pulled a second chair over beside his mother. "Okay, Mom. I know Isobel's time is limited. Let me tell you why I think you should go to Pine Ridge this time around. Then you can tell me how you feel about it."

Isobel gave him an approving nod. They'd talked more than once about letting their parents make as many decisions as they could themselves to give them control over their lives.

He handed his mother the two brochures and while she examined them, he asked Isobel in a low voice, "How did your meeting with Kane go?"

Isobel looked disconcerted for a minute, maybe even a little guilty, but then she replied, "It went all right. But we were interrupted again. My sister needed me and I had to leave."

"I'm sorry. Anything serious?"

"No. Chad's bus broke down on the way home from the game and she needed me to babysit while she went to get him."

"So when do you talk to Kane again?"

"I'm not sure. Maybe at the end of the week. He said he has interviews lined up back-to-back for the next few days."

West frowned. "Yeah, I know. I'm one of them. Is he tough?"

"I don't know if *tough*'s the word. But his questions *are* pointed. And he doesn't like it when his interviewee hedges."

"That's what you tried to do?"

"*Tried* is the operative word," Isobel said with a small smile. "I'm sure we all feel a little defensive, but he cuts right through that."

From the bed, Florence pointed to the one brochure. "I like the one with the blue rooms and the dining room where everyone eats together."

West smiled. "That's Pine Ridge and that's my choice, too."

Somehow this was all going to work out. Then he could stop worrying about his mother and the rest of her golden years.

"Wait up," a now-familiar male voice called from the fourth-floor landing as Isobel hurried down the stairs. For the past few days she'd used the staircase at the back of the hospital, having decided the exercise would be much better for her.

Apparently Neil used the stairs, too. She waited halfway down the flight as he joined her. "Are the elevators too slow for you?" he asked with a smile.

"And sometimes too crowded. I was thinking about everything else I had to do this afternoon and didn't want to get caught up in a conversation."

When he frowned, she said quickly, "I didn't mean I don't want to talk to *you*."

"If you need to think, we can take the rest of the steps in companionable silence," he joked.

If he was walking beside her, she wouldn't be *able* to think.

"Thanks again for bringing my dad over to my sister's and buying the pizza."

"Your father's an interesting man. I enjoy talking with him."

She cocked her head. "What does *your* dad do?"

After a moment's hesitation, he answered her. "My father's a judge."

A judge who didn't get along with his son? "How long has he been a judge?" she asked, curious to know more about Neil's background.

"Since I was a teenager."

"Was that tough?"

Neil's expression, open and friendly before, was now closed and guarded. "I'd rather not talk about my father."

"I'm sorry. I just thought since we were talking about mine—" She didn't know where to go from there and now she felt awkward. "Never mind." She turned away from Neil and started down the stairs again.

But he caught her arm and was beside her before she could take another breath. "I told you, I'm not close to my family like you are to yours. Talking about the reasons why doesn't change anything."

She could tell him that talking might give him another perspective. She could tell him that talking *with* his family might even be better.

"I can hear the wheels turning," he said seriously. "I know in your professional position, you're good at mediation and counseling. But I don't want any counsel. And mediation isn't something my father would ever consider. So let's drop it."

"Sure," she murmured feeling unreasonably hurt.

She had no right to feel hurt. Neil Kane was nothing to her. They'd shared a few conversations. They'd enjoyed an evening with her family. But they weren't involved and probably never would be. If Neil was guarded in this area, he was probably guarded in others. He was probably wounded from his divorce. He probably didn't feel attracted to her at all, not the way she felt attracted to him.

She was trying hard not to show any emotion, but something must have shown. He took a step closer and cupped her chin in his palm. "Isobel," he said softly, with such tenderness Isobel's throat felt tight.

He ran his thumb along her cheekbone and she trembled. She knew he could feel it.

"Damn," he growled. "I never get involved or even friendly with someone in my investigation."

His finger was still on her cheek and she could feel it touching someplace deep inside. "Because you lose perspective?" she wanted to know.

"Because the guilty can seem innocent and the innocent can seem guilty. I never take the chance that I'm wrong. I always go by the book. It was the way I was raised, the way I was taught and the way I've lived my life."

So his father had an influence even though Neil hadn't wanted him to? She didn't ask that question out loud because she was too lost in the heat in Neil's eyes, too lost in the way he was looking at her.

There was complete silence in the stairwell. The steel fire doors kept the busy noise in the halls from entering the staircase. Her heart was pounding in her ears, racing with anticipation and expectation.

Neil's hand slid to her neck under her curly hair. The warmth of his skin felt so good…the touch of his fingers against her scalp so sensually right. When he tilted her head up and lowered his, she knew exactly what was going to happen. He paused just an instant in case she wanted to back away. She knew she *should* back away, but she definitely didn't want to. Curiosity and need were much stronger than any sense of propriety, or any admonition from her good sense that she was consorting with the enemy. Right now, Neil didn't feel like the enemy and she refused even to consider the fact that he might be.

It had been almost three years since she'd been kissed by a man…three years since she'd had any intimate contact at all. When Neil's lips touched hers, she savored the sensation, recognizing the chemistry that was stronger than any she'd ever experienced. She could shyly wait to see what he'd do next but she didn't. Her arms went around his neck and when they did, his tongue slid into her mouth. The material of his suit coat was smooth against her arms. His hair was thick and coarse under her fingers. The scent of his cologne and something more basic intoxicated her until she forgot she was a social worker who worked for Walnut River General and she became totally a woman in Neil Kane's arms.

When his tongue probed her mouth, she stroked against it and heard him groan. Pressed together on the narrow step, they hardly moved for fear they'd teeter off. But Neil's tongue moved, his hand on her back moved, and she pressed into him seeking his arousal, proving she was as hungry as he was. After his hands crept up and down her back, they settled in her hair. His fingers tangled in her curls as if they couldn't get enough of the feel of them.

Abruptly—all too soon—his hands stilled and he broke away. "I feel like a teenager in high school between classes."

She almost lost her balance and his arms went around her again. "Are you okay?"

"Just fine," she lied, still in a daze from the erotic sensations running through her.

"We wouldn't want anyone to see us together like this," he said somberly.

"No, we wouldn't," she agreed thinking about her career, her friendships, Neil's investigation.

"That's been an event waiting to happen since the moment we met."

Apparently he'd felt the sparks, too. Now that it had happened, she didn't know quite how to put her feelings into words. Taking a deep breath, she ran a hand through her hair, straightened her jacket, and pasted on a smile. "I have to get to Admissions. I have a meeting there in…" She checked her watch. "Ten minutes."

"I was on my way to X-ray. There are some reports there I need to look over."

She knew better than to ask questions because Neil wouldn't answer them.

They began descending the steps together but this time they didn't converse, and this time the silence wasn't companionable. There was too much electricity still crackling between them, too much uncertainty about what had happened and what should happen next.

When they stood silently on the first-floor landing, Neil pulled open the heavy fire door and Isobel preceded him through it. She heard voices right away—raised voices—just around the corner. She recognized them.

"I can't make Anna see reason any more than *you* can," Peter Wilder said to his brother David.

"Can't you talk sense into her?" David asked Ella. "You two used to be so close."

"*Used to be* is the operative phrase," Ella responded sadly. "Ever since she quit med school, too much distance has grown between us. It's partially my fault, partially the family's fault. I think Anna feels like an outsider with us because she's different in so many ways."

"Maybe so," David agreed. "But that doesn't excuse her now, working for a company that's trying to destroy Dad's legacy."

Peter added, "She doesn't see it that way. In fact, she

insists if Northeastern HealthCare takes over, we'll have access to the latest research and technology. She doesn't realize how the company's deluding her."

"They're in it for the money," David insisted. "And as long as she's working *for* them, she's working *against* us. Dad's lifelong pursuits and our careers don't seem to mean anything to her anymore."

Neil clasped Isobel's elbow and whispered in her ear, "We've got to let them know we're here." Taking a step back, he opened and closed the stairway door once more, letting it bang loudly.

The conversation around the corner stopped. Neil guided Isobel toward the Wilders. Ella smiled at Isobel. David eyed Neil suspiciously. Peter just looked resigned.

They would have walked by the Wilder clan, but Peter called out, "Isobel, may I speak with you?"

When Neil released her arm, she felt the absence of his touch. Neil nodded at Peter then his gaze met Isobel's. His expression was neutral but there was still heat in his eyes, heat that she felt, too. "I'll call your office soon," he said, "and we'll finish up with those questions." He didn't look back as he strode down the hall, leaving her with Peter Wilder.

"Everything okay?" Peter asked her, his gaze still on Neil's back.

"Everything's fine." If you could count being kissed senseless as being fine, she thought.

"Do you think you could clear a few minutes in your schedule for me? There's something I need to discuss with you. I'm tied up tomorrow. Thursday I have more wiggle room."

Isobel mentally went over her schedule for the week. There was never enough time in a day but she could give Peter a few minutes of her lunch hour. "I can see you at twelve-thirty on Thursday unless there's an emergency."

"That sounds good, thanks. Can you come to my office?"

Isobel knew that something had been troubling Peter lately. She'd assumed it was the takeover attempt and now the investigation. But maybe there was something else, something more personal. Whatever it was, she hoped she could help him with it. "Sure. I'll call you if something comes up."

After Peter turned away, Isobel hurried toward Admissions, all the while not thinking about Peter or the discussion she'd overheard with his family. Only one thing filled her mind—Neil's kiss and how she'd felt when she'd kissed him back.

"You're better than I thought you'd be," Chad muttered as Neil prevented another of the sixteen-year-old's shots from flying into the basket.

They were playing basketball in Chad's driveway and Neil was enjoying it. He'd been surprised when Isobel's nephew had phoned him earlier and asked if he'd like to shoot some hoops. Neil had agreed, knowing he could use the exercise, suspecting Chad wanted some older male company. He obviously missed his dad.

"We're even. I can't let you drop another one in," Neil insisted as a car drew up at the curb. It was Isobel's car.

He and Chad were hard at it again when Isobel walked up the driveway and stopped to watch them. "This is a surprise." Just that moment of inattention, of listening to her voice, was all Chad needed to score on Neil.

"I won," Chad crowed, then did something unexpected. He tossed the ball to Isobel.

She easily caught it.

"Want to play, Aunt Iz? I've got homework to do."

Isobel must have stopped at home before coming over.

She was dressed in jeans, a sweatshirt and running shoes. "Maybe Neil's not up for another game. You might have tired him out."

He could hear the mischief in Isobel's tone. She was daring him to play basketball with her. He never turned away from a dare. "We have a half hour of daylight left. I've got enough energy left to make eleven before you see five."

"You're on." She threw the ball to Neil and, taking her shoulder bag from her arm, she tossed it to Chad. "Take that inside, would you?"

Her nephew saluted, grinned and loped off. Isobel's fingers went to the waistband of her sweatshirt.

Neil found himself holding his breath as she pulled it up and over her head, revealing a red T-shirt that fitted snugly against her breasts and defined her waist. The next thing he knew, she'd pulled a headband out of her pocket and slipped it on. She looked too sexy for words. His mouth went dry and he didn't know how he was going to guard her when he'd much rather pull her into the garage and kiss her blind. He hadn't been able to forget their encounter in the stairwell— not one little detail of it.

"Ready when you are," she said sweetly.

He tossed the ball back to her. "Try to make a basket."

As they did a side dance, first to the left and then to the right, she asked, "So what are you doing here?"

When she tried to throw, he easily blocked her, snatched the ball, pivoted on one foot and shot. The ball swooped through the basket.

Catching it on a bounce, he handed it to her. "Try again." When she didn't move, he replied, "Chad called me and asked if I wanted to play basketball. I'd given him my card last night. Since I needed the exercise, I said yes."

Isobel dribbled thoughtfully. "He needs a male role model."

"How often does he see his dad?"

"Not often enough. A week in the summer, every other holiday." Craftily she slipped under Neil's arm and made a basket.

"So you're going to be sneaky," he teased.

"I aim to win."

"Not if I can help it."

They went at their game seriously then.

After Neil had scored two and Isobel one, he spotted the determination in her eyes. She was going to try to mow him down. He could have moved out of the way. He could have simply blocked her with one long arm. But the devil inside him made him stand perfectly still as he took her shoulder into his chest. She pushed and he didn't push back. Her curls were damp around her face, her breath was coming quick and hard, her breasts pushed into him and his arm came around her, holding her still. The ball fell from her hand, bounced and rolled away. When she looked up at him, the sizzle that had begun the moment they'd met snapped and sparked.

"I've got to…" she stopped. "I've got to get the ball."

"We could try another kiss instead of playing basketball," he suggested, his voice huskier than he'd like.

Instead of considering that option seriously, Isobel pushed a curl from her cheek, stepped back and responded, "My sister would ask too many questions if we did that."

"Maybe the questions would be worth it," he remarked.

"Maybe another kiss would take us somewhere we don't want to go." She looked as serious as he'd ever seen her and he knew she'd meant what she said.

"I'll get the ball." He needed to move before he took her

into his arms and kissed her into oblivion, making her wish they'd never stop.

The ball had rolled off the tarmacadam to the side of the garage where Chad's bike stood tilted against the forsythia bush.

Isobel came over and laid her hand over the seat on the racing bike.

"It's a nice bike." His comment was lame, but he needed something to get them back on easy footing.

"Chad's father gave it to him for his birthday. He told him to go down to the bike shop and pick out the one he wanted."

Neil stood by her shoulder, watching the shadows from falling dusk play over her face. "You sound as if you don't approve."

"Chad likes the bike and he knows his mom never could have afforded one like it. But the truth is, he would have appreciated his dad flying in here and spending a weekend with him a lot more."

Playing devil's advocate, Neil offered, "Airfare's expensive."

"If you have kids, they should come first, foremost and always," she said vehemently.

"You mean when *you* have kids that's what will happen."

"I think that's what should happen for every child. And yes, when I have children, I'll put them first."

He knew he was stepping into private territory but had to ask, "You want children?"

She looked down at the bike then up at him. "Very much. How about you?"

"I'd like to have kids someday. I've often thought about joining a Big Brother program."

"Why haven't you?"

"Because when I make a promise or a commitment, I believe in keeping it. My job sometimes takes me away unexpectedly and I wouldn't want to have to break a planned trip to a ball game or a movie or a day at the park. That wouldn't be fair."

"You said you believe in keeping promises and commitments. How did you look at getting a divorce?" As soon as she asked the question, her cheeks turned red and she shook her head. "Never mind. I'm sorry, I shouldn't have asked that."

If anyone else had asked, he probably would have gotten angry. But Isobel... He knew she wasn't making a judgment, she just wanted to know.

He slid his hands into his jeans pockets, gazed down the treelined street then answered her. "My marriage to Sonya never should have happened. I don't know how much in love we were. We met after I quit the Boston P.D. We liked each other. I think we saw marriage as a convenient way to get on with our lives."

He brought his gaze back to Isobel now. "But she didn't anticipate how much I'd be away. I didn't know how much I didn't want to share myself with anyone. Your father was right last night. Although neither of us understood what we were doing, we set boundaries we didn't want to cross. Since then, I've realized a couple can't have boundaries like that. They have to be willing to go deep into each other's territory, even if it's uncomfortable, and even if it hurts. Sonya and I weren't willing to do that, so we were never as close as we should have been. Eventually closeness became something we avoided."

The furrow between his brows deepened when he added, "In spite of that, I was committed to her and to our marriage.

But she was lonely, and she found someone who would make her feel less lonely. So to answer your question, I rationalized. I told myself she broke our vows first by being unfaithful. But in reality, maybe I broke our vows first by isolating myself from her."

"You've thought a lot about this," Isobel remarked quietly.

"I don't like to fail at anything. That's not the way I'm made. I grew up believing success was the bar every man should use to determine whether he's had a good life."

"We learn more when we fail than when we succeed," she suggested.

"You're a deep thinker, aren't you?" he asked.

She smiled wryly. "I'm not sure that's a compliment."

"Sure it is. You don't just consider the surface, but what's *below* the surface."

The screen door slammed. Chad jogged to where they were standing by his bike.

"We were just admiring it," Neil told him.

"I remembered I didn't put it away. I have to be careful and chain it up wherever I take it."

"Unlike *my* bike," Isobel teased him. "Nobody would want it."

"Do you ride much?" Neil asked.

Before she could answer, Chad did. "She used to ride at least ten miles every day. But she doesn't have time since she moved in with Grandpa. Do you ride?" Chad asked Neil.

"I used to. Now I spend more time on the life cycle at the gym than on a real bike."

"If you want to use mine to go riding with Aunt Iz, you can."

"I'll think about that," Neil assured him.

As Chad wheeled his bike around to the side door of the

garage, he called over his shoulder, "Mom said she baked a chocolate cake today. It's on the table whenever you're ready." Once Chad had taken the bike inside the garage, Neil realized the sun was setting and in a few minutes, the shadows would turn to darkness.

"We could go riding sometime," he said casually. It wasn't so much an invitation as a gambit to see what Isobel would say.

She shook her head. "That's probably not a good idea."

"Because we're on opposite sides?"

"Because your job is still the main priority in your life and when this investigation is over, you'll be headed for the next one."

She was right. If it weren't for his job—

Would he still be married?

Would he have kids?

Would he be living in the suburbs with a picket fence and a minivan?

"You're a planner, aren't you, Isobel? When you take a first step, you want to know what the next one will be."

"Is there anything wrong with that?" She sounded a bit defensive.

"I just wonder if you're not missing out on joy and excitement along the way."

"I'm not a risk taker."

"I'm sorry you're not." He'd like to get to know her better. He'd like to take more than a bike ride with her, but he could see she wasn't even going to give them the chance to enjoy a few hours together. He represented danger to her—danger because the risk of getting involved with him would only hurt her. He couldn't blame her for wanting to keep her heart safe, but he was filled with regret that they wouldn't be taking a step past the first kiss.

"I guess we'll have to call our game a draw," he decided.

"You were ahead," she reminded him.

"Being ahead doesn't mean I won."

"Neil, I wish—"

Before she could move away, he hung his arm around her shoulders, ignoring the stirring in his body that told him he wanted a hell of a lot more than the casual contact. "Don't wish. You have to be true to what's right for you. In the meantime, we'll eat chocolate cake and have a damn good time doing it."

He thought her eyes looked unnaturally moist but with darkness falling, it was hard to tell. As he guided her inside, he felt as if he'd lost something important to him.

Because of his past?

Because of his job?

Or because he still wasn't ready to open his heart?

Chapter Five

Isobel was out of breath as she braked to a stop on her bike in front of the Walnut River Inn. When she'd started out, she'd really had no intention of coming here.

Neil might not even be here.

She could just tell him she'd been out for an evening ride and…what? She just *happened* to pass the Inn?

She was almost ready to turn around and head down the street when she heard, "Isobel."

That was Neil's voice. He was standing on the porch wearing black jeans and a red polo shirt that seemed to emphasize his broad shoulders. His sandy-brown hair blew in the breeze. She couldn't see the color of his eyes from here but she knew their golden depths were trained on her.

He was coming down the steps now and she couldn't

pretend she didn't hear him call her. Wheeling her bike up the curved path, she parked it beside the porch.

"Hey," he said with a smile. "Did you just happen to be passing by, or did you come for a reason?"

Leave it to Neil to be blunt. When he wanted to know something, he just asked.

"I don't think that was a difficult question," he remarked, grinning now.

She felt foolish. Her hair was damp from her exertion but she had chosen a crisp yellow cotton blouse and her best pair of jeans to ride in. "Both, I guess. I didn't particularly have this destination in mind when I started out."

"If you want to talk, we can go up to my room. Or if you'd rather, we could go for a walk. But then, of course, some of the fine citizens of Walnut River might see you with me."

Pulling her helmet from her head, she hung it on her handlebars. Should she go to his room? This conversation would be short, and at least they'd be able to discuss things in private. "Do you have any water in your room?"

"In fact, I have a small refrigerator stocked with juice, soda *and* water."

She wasn't afraid of Neil. He was the kind of man a woman could trust. No, she hadn't been around him that much, but she did have sensitive radar in her line of work. "Juice would be terrific."

Opening the door, he led the way through the foyer and to the staircase. She admired the hardwood banister, the fine-quality blue-and-white wallpaper.

Neil had let her go first and at the head of the stairs, he directed her, "Second room on the left."

Neil was staying in the Lighthouse Room. It overlooked the backyard with its profusion of bushes and trees, which were all green with spring life. But she hadn't come here to admire the inn or the nautical décor in the room. She could see Neil had made himself at home. His laptop was open on the small blue desk and there was a stack of papers beside it. He was wearing deck shoes but sneakers were tumbled haphazardly under a straight-back chair next to the double bed. On the nightstand, a psychological thriller lay open next to the phone.

She'd come here tonight for a reason and one reason only. "I think we should talk about what happened in the stairwell."

Neil closed the door and the little click made her realize how alone they were, and more aware of how attracted she was to him—his height, the sandy hair on his forearms, his strong chin. He motioned to the red upholstered chair by the window, but she shook her head.

"So I guess this is going to be a short conversation," he remarked glibly.

"How can you joke—"

"I'm not joking, Isobel. Apparently you came to get something out of the way. You just want to do it and go on home again. No muss, no fuss."

He sounded almost angry and she had no idea why. "I don't want to take up any more of your time than I have to. And for your information I'm working on a fund-raising auction for the senior center. We have two more weeks to get donations and there's still a lot to do."

"Then why do we need to talk about the kiss at all?"

"Because…because it affects our interaction together—professionally," she added quickly.

"Oh, you mean whenever you see me at the hospital, you're going to think about the kiss?"

"Why are you making this so difficult?" She really was puzzled.

"Tell me something. Are you and Peter Wilder involved?"

"No." Isobel was so shocked she couldn't think of anything else to say.

"When I left the two of you, you looked pretty chummy."

"Peter is engaged to Bethany. They're getting married next month."

Neil's expression didn't change.

Now *she* was getting mad, too. "Do you honestly think I'd even be tempted to get involved with someone who is already promised to someone else?"

When he didn't answer, she had had enough. "If you do think that," she headed for the door, "I shouldn't be here at all."

He caught her arm. "Isobel, wait. No, I don't think that. But you seemed very friendly with Wilder."

"Are you digging now? For professional reasons, or personal ones?"

He frowned and admitted, "Personal ones."

She could see that Neil was serious, that maybe after their kiss he'd even been a little bit jealous. That idea made her heart flutter faster. "Peter and I…" She stopped and shook her head. "We're colleagues."

"And you can't say more than that because he's perhaps consulting you about something?"

She kept silent.

Releasing her arm, he placed a hand on both her shoulders and nudged her a little closer. "So…" he drawled. "What did *you* want to talk about?"

After a shaky breath, she laid it out. "I can't get involved with you. There's no point. Not when you'll be leaving after a few weeks."

"Isobel," he said in a soft, gentle voice that made her name sound romantic. "Have you ever taken a roller-coaster ride?"

Her eyes widened because she absolutely didn't know where he was going with this question. "Actually no, I never have."

His brows arched and he rubbed his thumb back and forth over her collar bone, distracting her immensely. "You don't know what you're missing. As an amusement-park ride, it's meant for fun and excitement and thrills. You start out slowly and you think, *Oh, this isn't so scary,* but then you start mounting the first hill. The excitement builds. You're still going very slowly but although the earth is far below, you don't seem to be in any danger. But then you come to the top of the hill. It seems like you're suspended there for a moment, just a moment, and then, so fast that you don't know what hit you, you're over the top, down the dip, on a straight stretch into another dip, up another hill, down with a whoosh. There's absolutely nothing like it, except maybe a kiss like we shared. Except maybe *thinking* about another kiss."

"Neil," she protested softly.

He nudged her a little closer and at the same time, he moved in, too. "Tell me you don't want to experience another dip and whoosh."

"Fun and excitement and thrills have never been driving forces in my life." She practically squeaked because she was so deprived of air.

"Maybe it's time to change that."

Getting hold of herself, she managed to ask, "How many affairs have you had since your divorce?"

Now it was his turn to look startled. "I thought *I* asked tough questions," he commented wryly.

She waited.

"I'm not a thrill-seeker either, Isobel. I've only dated two other women since my divorce."

If he was telling her the truth, that information truly astonished her. "Two women in two years?"

"I've gone out with a few others, but nothing developed from it. I don't take every woman I date to bed. I'm careful, I'm selective, and to be honest, I work too much to have a social life."

"So you see me as a diversion from your job?"

"No, Isobel. I see you as someone special. The moment you walked into my office, I felt it. Didn't you?"

If she admitted that—

"I thought it was a fluke," he went on. "I thought I'd been cooped up for too long, asked too many questions, interviewed too many personnel. So when an attractive woman walked in, sure, she got my attention, but then minute by minute, that current between us never subsided. By the time you left, I was having a hell of a time keeping my mind on what I was supposed to be asking you."

"You could have fooled me."

"Yeah, well, usually I'm great at compartmentalizing. I can separate the work from my personal life. That's why I've never dated anyone involved in a case."

"Never?"

"Never."

"So…are you considering dating me?"

He laughed. "Dating? Let's put it this way. I'd like to spend more time with you."

"And what about the investigation?"

"I've been doing this a long time, Isobel. You're not involved in anything going on at the hospital. *If* something is going on. In fact, I think you could be a help to me."

"What kind of help?"

"I'd like you to go through some of the files and computer data with me and answer questions I might have. No one else is willing to do that, either because they don't want to get the hospital in trouble, or because they do. I can't trust either side because of the takeover issue. But I think you would be honest with me. You're an insider. You know the goings-on. I think you could be an asset. No one has to know you're helping me if we do it in our off-hours."

"You really trust me that much?"

"I do."

Could he be playing her? Could he be using her? Could he be telling her he trusted her to get her to trust him?

"So many suspicions," he said with a rueful shake of his head. "Maybe this will help prove I'm telling the truth."

She'd thought about Neil's kiss since it had happened. She hadn't been able to think about much else. But now she had the opportunity to kiss him again. Did she want to take that roller-coaster ride? Did she want to change her life and put a few thrills in it?

Staring into Neil's forthright brown eyes, she simply couldn't resist the romantic notion that he was attracted to her, or the excitement of being desired.

She lifted her lips and he didn't hesitate. His kiss took her back to the stairwell and then sent her head spinning. His tongue was so erotically sensual, all she could do was hold on, breathe in his scent, feel his strength and ask for more. Not in words, but by stroking his tongue, by pressing her breasts against his chest, by letting her leg settle between his.

He groaned, pressed her even closer, then broke the kiss and lifted his head. "Damn it, Isobel. If you don't want to end up in that bed, we've got to stop now."

She almost smiled—almost—though her heart was still racing, her body still tingling. Neil was looking at her as if she *were* "special." That was almost hard to take, hard to accept, hard to feel because she'd never felt that kind of special with a man before. Finally the haze of sensual hunger diminished as each second ticked by.

She backed away from him another step. "I'd better go."

"You didn't have your juice."

"I'd better go," she said again.

His face was stoic now as he nodded and let her precede him out the door. They didn't speak as he walked her down the steps, as they made their way through the foyer and out over the front threshold.

He looked as if he might want to kiss her again. She knew if she let him do that, they'd end up back in his room, on his bed, *in* his bed.

She descended the porch steps.

"Isobel."

She turned to look at him.

"Will you help me?"

There was only one rule of thumb she used to guide her actions. Not what other people thought, not what her friends might say, not even what her coworkers might do. It was something her mother and dad had taught her well. She always tried to do what was right. And helping Neil get to the bottom of the hospital's problems seemed *right*.

"Yes," she said softly.

Without looking at him again, without witnessing a desire in his eyes he couldn't quite bank, without feeling the yearning for yet another kiss, she flipped up her kickstand, wheeled her bike to the sidewalk, hopped on and rode away.

* * *

The following afternoon, Isobel stopped by Peter's office, curious as to why he wanted to see her.

"I suppose you didn't eat lunch," he began.

"I blocked off this time for you today. I'll grab something later."

"I know the hours you put in. Everyone here appreciates that."

"You're not chief of staff anymore," she reminded him with a smile.

"No, I guess I'm not. Some habits are hard to break. I still care too much about this hospital and everyone in it."

"Can you care *too* much?"

Peter ran his hand through his dark-brown hair. "I try to put the investigation and the takeover bid out of my head when I'm seeing patients. But those are always there, like swords hanging over my head."

"Is that why you wanted to talk to me?"

He leaned back and took a deep breath. Then he pulled a letter out of the inside of his suit jacket. "No. I want to talk to you about something my father left."

She could see the legal-size envelope had the name *Anna* written on it. As was Isobel's usual habit, she didn't poke or prod. She let Peter set the pace.

"I've had this since my father's estate was settled. His lawyer gave it to me."

"Something for Anna?"

"It's a letter within a letter. My dad wrote to me explaining what this letter was, that he wanted me to make the decision of whether to give it to her. It's one hell of a responsibility."

"Do you know what it says?"

"Not explicitly. But it does explain to her that she's our *half* sister, not our *adopted* sister."

"That must have been difficult for you to learn."

"It was. But even more shocking…" He paused for a moment, then went on. "My father had an affair and my mother never knew about it. Anna was the result of that affair."

"That *is* a bombshell. It was a huge secret for your father to keep. And now you're considering keeping it, too?"

"It's really Anna's secret. Still, I don't like keeping something so important from David and Ella, either."

"So if you give this letter to Anna, would you be giving it to her for *her* sake or for your sake?"

He smiled wryly. "This is exactly why I wanted to talk to you. To try and figure that out."

"I'm sure it isn't anything you haven't thought of already."

"No, I guess it isn't. I just don't know what to do, Isobel, because of the tension with Anna right now. She works for the company that wants to destroy everything my father spent his life building! At least that's the way Ella, David and I see it."

"That's business, not personal," Isobel reminded him.

"You think the two can be separated?"

"Maybe not in *your* mind, but maybe in Anna's mind they can."

"I can understand if she wants to be loyal to the company that pays her, but that's clashing with *family* loyalty."

"If you give her this letter, what do you think it will do?"

"It will either put her on the family's side, or make her stand even firmer against us because of what my father did and never acknowledged. I have to ask myself how I would feel having lived in a house all those years with a man who claimed to be my adopted father, yet who was my *real* father and he never told me."

"Do you believe it's better if she never knows?"

"I don't know what I believe, except that a secret carries weight and that weight is a burden. On the other hand, I can't believe a person wouldn't want to know the truth about their life, their parents, their real family. How can I possibly keep that information from her?"

Isobel let the question hang in the air.

"I guess I knew the answer all along, didn't I? But I just can't spring this on Anna, either. I'm going to have to find the right time to give it to her."

"You'll know the right time," Isobel assured him.

Peter stood and so did Isobel. "Thank you for stopping in. I just needed to…lay it all out in front of someone objective."

"Have you told Bethany?"

"Yes. We don't have secrets. But she can't be objective because she loves me." He grinned. "I wouldn't trade that for anything."

"I wouldn't, either," Isobel agreed.

As she moved toward the door, Peter asked, "You *are* coming to our wedding, aren't you? The invitations go out next week."

"I wouldn't miss it."

After a goodbye and Peter's thanks, Isobel left his office and passed his exam rooms, going through the door to the reception area. Five minutes later, she was back at her office. To her surprise, she found Neil waiting for her.

"You just happened to be passing by?" she teased as she unlocked the knob, her fingers fumbling with the key.

He took the key from her hand. "Want me to try?" He was so very close to her, his arm brushing hers, his fit body a reminder of how she'd felt pressed against him.

He easily slid the key into the lock and opened the door. Then he followed her inside.

"I thought we could work on the files tonight," he explained. "Your place or mine? I'll spring for dinner."

"I put stew in the slow cooker this morning. It will be ready when I get home. Do you want to come over to my dad's place?"

"Are you sure he won't mind someone barging in?"

"I'm positive. So much of what I do is confidential and I can only talk about it in broad terms. Dad gets tired of that. He likes specifics. Unless I've gotten an e-mail from Jacob or something new happens with Debbie, our dinner conversation is pretty dull."

"What would we do without the weather?" Neil asked, sounding serious.

"That's what you talk about with your parents, too?"

"Yeah, that's the main topic of conversation. Why don't I stop at that bakery on Lexington and pick up something for your dad's sweet tooth. What's his favorite?"

"Anything with chocolate."

"Is chocolate your favorite, too?"

The timbre of his voice created pictures in her mind of satin sheets, naked bodies, strawberries dipped in chocolate and whipped cream. "Like father, like daughter," she answered flippantly.

Neil dragged his finger from her cheek to the corner of her lip. He looked as if he wanted to kiss her, but he knew where they were and so did she. "I'll meet you at home."

When she nodded, Isobel knew deep down that she was just asking for trouble and she didn't care.

It was so obvious to Isobel that her father liked Neil. Throughout dinner they talked and Isobel enjoyed just sitting there and listening, seeing her father totally engaged. After she had cleared the table, her father watched Neil set up his laptop computer.

"So you're both going to work now?" he grumbled.

"Isobel's going to help me go through some files," Neil explained.

"And you don't want anyone at the hospital to know you're helping him, do you?" her dad asked her.

Isobel and Neil exchanged a look. Both of them wondered how much her father knew. To distract her dad, Neil asked him, "Have you ever worked on a computer?"

John frowned, apparently knowing full well what Neil was doing. "I sold out my hardware business before I had to computerize. Ledgers were always good enough for me. I didn't need a machine that could make everything disappear with the tap of one wrong key."

"I think you might like where the Internet could take you, especially with your love of history."

"What does history have to do with it?"

"You could find sites devoted to any subject you wanted to read about. Some senior centers are setting up computer banks and teaching seniors how to use them." Neil glanced at Isobel. "You said you're helping with an auction to raise funds for the senior center. It would be a project to suggest."

"Would you be interested in something like that, Dad?" Isobel asked, curious.

"You mean I could look up Eisenhower or Truman or Thomas Jefferson?"

"You certainly could. Do you go to the senior center? You could ask your friends if they'd be interested."

"I haven't gone since I had this shoulder operated on."

"You know Mr. Bruckenwalt told you he'd pick you up and take you whenever you wanted to go," Isobel reminded him.

"It's bad enough Cyrus has to take me to and from PT. I'm not going to ask him to chauffeur me to the senior center. Besides, I can't even lift my own lunch tray yet. A man's got his pride."

"Your pride is keeping you cooped up in here. That's why you're bored," Isobel offered gently.

"Do you miss your friends?" Neil asked.

Her dad shrugged, not wanting to admit it. "I keep myself occupied. I do crossword puzzles. Now that the weather is nicer, I can take walks."

"And soon you're going to be using that arm again," Isobel said encouragingly.

"You and your positive thinking. Sometimes it makes a man tired." He sank down heavily into his recliner.

"When you went to the senior center, what did you do there?" Neil asked.

"Ate lunch, played cards, yakked about the old days."

"Is there any reason why you can't invite some of your friends here? You could order a pizza. You wouldn't have to worry about carrying a tray."

Isobel's dad was silent for a few moments.

"I never thought about doing that. I know Benny doesn't like to go to the senior center anymore, either, because he can't hear very well. He might like to come over, too."

"We've got at least three decks of cards in the desk drawer," Isobel commented nonchalantly, thinking Neil's idea was a good one.

"Yeah, we do, don't we?" Her dad rubbed his chin and pushed himself out of the recliner. "Maybe I'll call Benny now and see what he thinks. Then I'll turn in for the night. You two aren't going to be any fun if you're going to work."

Her dad smiled at them to take the sting out of his words, then headed for the stairs.

After she could hear her dad's footsteps in the upstairs hall, Isobel sat down next to Neil on the sofa. "I wish I had thought of your suggestion. I don't know why I didn't."

"You've had a lot on your plate. One person can't think of everything."

Their gazes met and held for one very long minute. Neil had tossed his suit coat over the back of the sofa and tugged off his tie. His white oxford shirt was rumpled from a day of wear, but with the cuffs rolled back, he looked incredibly relaxed—and sexy. The temperature in the room seemed to climb another ten degrees. With the warmer weather, the house was a little stuffy.

"Do you need to be hooked up to the phone line?" she asked him.

"No, I have everything on the flash drive. I just need an outlet. Why?"

"Because we could go out on the sunporch and work. I can open the window."

"That sounds like a great idea. Grab my briefcase. I'll get the computer."

Five minutes later, they were set up on the glassed-in porch. The light beside the wicker sofa burned brightly. Darkness had fallen and the scent of just-blooming lilacs wafted in from the open window that looked out onto the backyard.

Side by side they sat there, breathing in the spring flowers and dampness, night settling in and each other. Oh, they worked. Neil brought up page after page that Isobel examined with him, searching for charges that didn't fit, checking anything that seemed over the top, showing him her own billing sheets. She explained basic charges, time allotments, services rendered.

Still, their arms brushed often, his shirtsleeve against her bare skin. When she pointed to something on the screen, he leaned close, his mouth almost touching her cheek. By the time they had spent an hour and a half examining and checking, silence and shadows and the perfumes of spring wrapped them in an intimate cocoon.

"This is tedious work," Isobel murmured as they finished another page.

"It's not so bad doing it with you." Neil's voice had a husky quality that brought her eyes to his. The desire she saw there made her breath catch and her mouth go dry.

After a moment she asked, "Would you like me to get us something to drink?"

"I'd like something else a lot more."

She didn't have to ask what Neil wanted because she wanted it, too. Leaning into him, she raised her lips to his.

Chapter Six

Time, place and consequences had no hold on Isobel as she gave herself up to the delight of Neil's kiss. That delight, however, soon morphed into desire and thrills and novelty that made her gasp in pleasure and moan in surrender.

The wicker couch's floral cushions gave with their weight as Neil's arms wrapped around her and they leaned against its back. His lips were on her cheek, on her eyelids, then they returned to her mouth. His hands smoothed over the back of her silky blouse then roamed into new territory. They were at her waist, on her stomach, almost touching her breasts.

Isobel's slim skirt rode up her thighs as she restlessly reached for handfuls of Neil's shirt and pulled it from his trousers. She didn't think twice about what they were doing. She didn't think at all. She'd never experienced such mindless pleasure or basked in a man's hungry desire. She and Tim—

well, they'd been attracted to each other, but she'd never wanted to put her hands all over him the way she wanted to put her hands all over Neil. She'd never wanted to get into Tim's skin the way she wanted to get into Neil's. She'd never before felt the heat and the urgency to make love because she knew when she did, she'd rocket straight away from earth. Neil had that effect on her, whether he was just looking at her, kissing her or touching her. There was an innate virility that poured from him—an alpha determination he couldn't keep in check. Yet he could be kind and gentle, too. That mixture in a man was totally irresistible.

He stroked her hair back from her face. "Do you want this, Isobel? Are you sure?"

Beyond rationality, her body cried out for more—more of touching, kissing, holding and most of all, completion. "I do," she murmured, reaching for his belt buckle.

She didn't stop to admit that the illicit nature of making love on the back porch with her father upstairs had an element of danger she found enticing. She'd never realized the extent of the excitement that danced around danger—the danger of being heard or found or seen.

Still, she knew the glassed-in porch was so separate from the rest of the house, so far away from her father's room, he couldn't possibly hear them. Once he went upstairs for the night, he didn't come down again. Those steps were hard on his knees. As far as neighbors…their yard was bordered by maples, spruce and oaks. There might be a stray cat lurking out there, but not much else. A spirea hedge surrounded the yard and gravel from the alley beyond would alert them to a neighbor taking a walk, or a car backing in for the night.

All of those thoughts were extraneous as she trembled while Neil undressed her…as he shrugged out of his shirt and she unzipped his fly. Naked on the sofa, Neil pulled her onto his lap, caressed her breasts and kissed her lips. She could feel his arousal beneath her thigh. He was hot and hard and big. The excitement he created had her reaching between them, stroking his stomach, moving lower. He slid forward with her on the cushion, turned her on his lap so she was facing and straddling him. She'd never made love like this…this was over-the-top exhilarating, tempting, brand-new.

They didn't speak. They were too busy nibbling, kissing, tasting.

Neil turned from her, grabbed his trousers, fished in a pocket for his wallet. Moments later he was pushing into her, she was melting around him and desire was a newly awakened hunger that made a need so far deep inside of her, she didn't know how she'd satisfy it.

But Neil did. His hands slipped under her buttocks and he pushed in deeper, farther, groaning as his own hunger was partially satisfied. His lips clung to hers, his tongue never stopped moving, his body rocked closer, his hands guided her movement and they created an irresistible friction. She pushed, he thrust, they rocked until her muscles tightened, her nerve endings lit up with excitement and her world shattered into a thousand pieces around her. In the throes of her orgasm, she felt Neil's final thrust, held him as he shuddered, and sighed when his lips broke from hers. He caught her tight against his chest.

But after a few moments, he leaned against the back of the sofa, taking her with him. Her heart was beating hard against his chest and she could feel the racing of his heart, too. The primitive pounding in her ears slowed as they began to breathe normally again. Their bodies were glazed with their exertion and she loved the scent of Neil…the scent of the two of them together. He held her for a very long time.

She was almost lulled by a happiness she'd never experienced until she started thinking again. Neil had been prepared with a condom. That wasn't so unusual, she guessed, lots of men were. Still…

"Do you always carry a condom in your wallet?"

He was silent and she didn't look up. Finally he inquired, "Why are you asking?"

Now she sat up and awkwardly disengaged herself from him. She should get dressed, but she had to know something first. "I'm trying to put two and two together and I'm getting five. You said you haven't slept with many women, only a few since your divorce. Was the condom old or new?"

"Because you're concerned you might get pregnant if it's old?" His voice was gruff.

"Because if it's new, I have to wonder if you planned this. If you want to keep me close so I'll help you. If you want to get me on your side so you can get the information you need."

"Isobel." Her name was a protest tinged with anger.

She went on anyway. "You said you never get involved with someone in an investigation. Why now? Why me?"

His thumb nudged her chin up so she was gazing into his eyes. "Are you so lacking in self-confidence you don't know how beautiful you are?"

Although she wanted to cover herself, she couldn't look away. Did he mean that?

"I haven't had men rushing to take me out."

"Then you haven't met the right men."

He *was* angry, but at least his anger was honest. She could tell that. Had tonight been as important to him as it was to her? Or could he separate emotion from pure physical desire? Perhaps tonight had just been about slaking that desire.

"I told you I don't do one-night stands," she murmured.

"So why did this happen tonight?" he asked reasonably. "You know I'm not staying in Walnut River. You know I'll be gone when the investigation's over."

"I got caught up in—"

"In desire? In passion? There's nothing wrong with that, Isobel."

"Yes, there is. When there's no commitment, it shouldn't happen. That's the way I was raised. I want what my parents had."

"Life's too short to wait forever for perfection."

The bitterness in his voice surprised her. "Perfection?"

His hands slashed through the air. "The right place, the right time, the right decade. For a few moments, Isobel, you and I had something special. Wasn't that good enough?"

"A few moments isn't enough for me."

Now Neil levered himself off the couch, turned aside, then grabbed his clothes. "You should take your special moments where you can get them."

There was pain under his proclamation and she wanted to know where it was coming from. His divorce? "I don't understand."

After a prolonged silence he finally responded. "My brother died when he was twelve. He never had the chance to wait for special moments. He never had the chance to live."

"Neil, I'm sorry."

Neil pulled on his trousers and buckled his belt. His fingers flew over the buttons of his shirt. "This is my fault. I knew you were a woman with traditional values. I just...I just let my libido wallop my good sense. It won't happen again." He looked at her. "But just for the record, Isobel. I had no ulterior motive. I wanted you because I'm attracted to you. And that has nothing to do with the investigation."

Isobel picked up her clothes, too, and shrugged into her blouse without her bra. But before she could even button it, Neil was completely dressed and had gathered his laptop and files. "I'll see you around the hospital."

She was confused, not sure of his motives and not sure of hers. She simply didn't know what to say.

She didn't have to say anything because he left without another word. She knew she wouldn't be seeing him at the hospital, not unless she searched him out. But what was the point? To help him? He didn't really need her help and she… she couldn't let him make love to her again without losing her heart.

She realized she wouldn't mind losing it. She just didn't want Neil to crush it.

On Monday morning at 7:00 a.m., Isobel stopped by Pine Ridge Rehab to peek in on Florence and see how she was adjusting since her move there last week.

West's mother was having breakfast. Florence's face lit up when she saw Isobel. "Did you come to have breakfast with me?"

"I already had breakfast." If she could count the glass of orange juice as breakfast. "So I'll just keep you company and find out how you like it here."

"The food's pretty good," Florence told her, taking another bite of her pancakes. "But you know what? They make me walk." She pointed to her walker. "I'm beginning to hate that thing."

Isobel smiled. "Soon you'll graduate to a cane and then to nothing at all."

"I'll have to be very careful when I go home."

Isobel went on alert. "Very careful of what?" she asked softly, not wanting to jar Florence out of her confiding mood.

The little woman took a piece of bacon, crunched on it a while, and answered, "A while back, I left a pot on the stove. It scared West. When he came home, he said he smelled something awful."

"What were you making?"

"I was cooking noodles and all the water burned away. He said if he hadn't come in when he did, we would have had a fire."

This was exactly the kind of thing Isobel was worried about. If Florence was becoming that forgetful that she would cause herself harm, she had to be watched. "Can you tell me something, Florence?"

"What would you like to know, dear?" Florence picked up her coffee cup and took a sip, then settled the cup back down again. She pushed her tray toward Isobel. "Are you sure you don't want a slice of bacon?"

"I'm sure, but thank you for asking." Isobel thought about how she should phrase her question. She didn't want it to be in any way threatening or even nosy, because then Florence would clam up. "When I was driving in this morning, I noticed the daffodils blooming. You have those in your garden, don't you?"

"Well, yes, I do. I love the smell. I have a favorite vase I use to put them in the middle of the kitchen table."

"Do you walk up and down your street very often? To see the flowers? It's good exercise, too."

"West doesn't like me going out alone for walks."

"He doesn't? Is he afraid you'll fall?"

Florence stared down at her pancakes for a long time. Finally in a small voice, she admitted, "One time when I took a walk outside, I ended up over on Maple and couldn't get back home. Mrs. Johnson was out for her walk and she saw me, so she showed me the way home."

"Did West know you'd gotten...lost?"

"Oh, yes. She told him and that's why he doesn't like me to leave the house when he's not there. But I do sometimes. I just don't tell him. The thing is, that'll be harder now. He's already found someone to stay with me when I go home. I guess she'll take walks with me."

So West *was* aware of the care his mother needed. Thank goodness.

Isobel checked her watch and stood. "I really have to be going."

"So soon?"

"I'm sure after breakfast you'll be starting your therapy and you'll be busy, too."

"I just want to get well."

As Isobel gave Florence a hug and said goodbye, she realized how coherent and lucid Florence had been today. Isobel hoped her good days kept outnumbering her bad ones.

Yesterday Isobel had taken a ride to the cemetery before going to dinner at Debbie's for Mother's Day. She had felt the loss of her mom all day. She was glad West was doing everything he could for Florence while he still had her to love.

Though Isobel had been busier than busy all day, her work load didn't prevent thoughts of Neil from sneaking in, from capturing her at the first unguarded moment, from lingering in her mind underneath everything else. When she least expected them, pictures of her and Neil popped into her head: as they sat side by side in her dad's sunporch, as they'd kissed, as Neil had undressed her, as she'd made love to him.

She also remembered every word she'd said to him…her accusation…his reply. Most of all, his comment about his brother. *He never had the chance to wait for special moments.*

Was it any wonder she was hesitant to see Neil again? His office was on the same floor as hers but on the other side of the building. It was well after six and personnel from the fourth floor had mostly gone home. Maybe Neil had left, too. Avoiding him, though, would only postpone the inevitable.

She stopped in the restroom to make sure her hair was in some semblance of order, to add a dash of lipstick, to make certain her flowered spring dress still looked presentable. Telling herself to stop stalling, she headed for Neil's office. As she glimpsed the closed door, she thought maybe he had left. Then she saw his shadow through the frosted-glass window, and she knocked.

His "Come in" could have been for anyone. After she turned the knob and stepped inside, Neil's head came up from his computer and his gaze locked to hers.

"Are you busy?" she asked, and as soon as she did, she understood what a totally silly question that was. Of course, he was busy. Papers were spread all over the table and he'd been typing something on his laptop.

He pressed a key, typed a few letters, and pressed another. "I have a few minutes. What can I do for you?"

He could kiss her again. He could tell her he understood her fears about getting involved with him. He could say he forgave her for making the wrong assumption.

She didn't know where to start, but she could see he wasn't going to help her. She walked over to the chair on the other side of the table from him, pulled it around the corner so she was facing him. She sat in it because her knees were wobbly.

He looked away, adjusted a few papers into a pile, and didn't bring his gaze back to hers.

To save them both any more uncomfortable moments, she said, "I'm sorry."

If she thought that would soften the set of his jaw, the guarded look in his eyes, she was wrong. "About what? You didn't do anything wrong. *I* was the one who should have known better. I should have stayed away from you."

If he *had* stayed away from her, she would never have known how beautiful making love could be. At least, that's what *she'd* been doing. "I'm sorry for what I thought and said."

He shifted in his chair, ran one hand agitatedly through his hair. "Did you honestly think I'd have sex with you to get information? And don't just tell me what you think I want to hear. I want the truth."

What *was* the truth? "On a deep level, I didn't think that. I never would have let anything happen if I had any real suspicions. But afterward, on another level, I was scared and unsure and regretful. Believing you just wanted to use me helped…it helped me push you away."

Maybe Neil wasn't used to that kind of honesty because he looked very surprised. "I can't believe you're admitting that."

"It's the truth."

His serious eyes searched her face and then he seemed to relax a bit. "I wanted you, Isobel. That's why I was carrying a new condom. But I was also afraid I'd taken advantage of you. I'm the one in a position of power and—"

"Says you," she cut in.

Surprised again, he smiled. "You think you have some power?"

"Of course, I do. I'm the one who decides what I do and who I do it with. Your position has nothing to do with that."

He grinned slyly and she felt her whole face heat up. "You know what I mean."

Leaning forward, he took her hand and looked down at it. "I don't want to hurt you. I don't want to push you into something that isn't right for you."

Now, with Neil simply holding her hand, she wasn't sure what was right for her and what wasn't. "Last night, you mentioned you had a brother who died. How long ago did that happen?"

Releasing her hand, he stood and went to look out the window at the grounds below. She had the feeling he wasn't seeing anything out there. "Is that something else you don't want to talk about…like your father?"

He glanced over his shoulder at her. "You listen too well and see too much."

She could tell him she'd been practicing for years, that listening well and seeing a lot was part of her job. Not only part of her job, but who she was. But she knew he didn't want to hear that.

After the silence had stretched a little longer, he answered her. "It was the summer before my senior year in high school. Garrett had just turned twelve. He'd gone fishing with a friend at the river. No one was sure exactly what happened, whether he lost his footing, or whether he and his friend were simply fooling around as boys do. But he got towed by a strong current and drowned."

Unable to stay across the room from him, Isobel rose to her feet and crossed to Neil. "I'm so sorry," she said again. "Was it just the two of you, no other brothers or sisters?"

Neil nodded and finally looked at her. "Just the two of us.

I was an only child, groomed to be the perfect son my father wanted, until Garrett was born when I was six. He and I were very different. No one could resist Garrett from the moment he was born."

Isobel filled in what Neil wasn't saying. "At six, your parents didn't feel you needed much attention, so the baby got it all?"

Neil shrugged. "I've got to admit, I was happy as an only child. I loved Garrett and would have done anything for him because I fell under his charm, too. He was a great kid, always happy, everybody's friend. But more than once, I wished he wasn't around."

"Oh, Neil, don't tell me you felt guilty when he died."

"Wouldn't *you* have felt guilty? I know it was irrational. I didn't have anything to do with what had happened, but I still felt responsible. If I had been with him that day instead of with *my* friends… He'd asked me to go along. But I wanted to hang with guys who were making college plans and telling the most popular girls about them. I grew up the day Garrett died. I started to learn what was important and what wasn't."

Her heart went out to the teenager Neil had been. She also realized he carried that sense of responsibility with him today.

"How did your parents react to losing Garrett?"

"They were never the same. Their marriage was never the same. My dad was never overly demonstrative or even generous with compliments. But after we lost Garrett, he became even more remote, closed off from Mom and me. God knows I tried to make up for their loss. I had concentrated on basketball and the debate team. Garrett ran track. So I added that to my schedule too. Even won a few trophies. But nothing seemed to impress my father. At first I intended to be a lawyer and follow in dad's footsteps, but then when I saw it didn't matter what I did, I decided to do what made me feel successful. That's why I joined the Boston P.D."

"Have you and your father ever talked about all this?"

Neil just shook his head. "He didn't seem to want to hear what I had to say."

"What did he say when you told him you weren't going to be a lawyer?"

"He said that he'd give the money he'd put aside for my law-school degree to a local scholarship fund."

"Did he know why you weren't becoming a lawyer? Or did he just see it as rebellion against what he wanted?"

"I don't know what he thought or how he felt. My mother knew I was tired of school and I wanted a real life. I got it. Being a detective showed me more than I ever wanted to see. When I hit thirty-eight, I wanted something different, maybe a life *with* someone. So I took the job with the state."

"And you like what you're doing?"

"I still like it, at least the gathering-evidence part of it. When I'm questioning someone, I'm pitting my mind against theirs. It's a challenge."

Neil was definitely a complicated man. No one went through life without baggage and he had his share. But she knew he was an honorable man. Her accusations had been defensive rationalization on her part.

The longer they stood there, the more heat she could feel surrounding them. Making love hadn't diminished it. In fact, it had hiked up the vibrations to a new level.

The look in Neil's eyes told her he was thinking about kissing her again, but he was restraining himself because she'd told him that wasn't what she'd wanted. She'd told him she didn't want an involvement.

What good can come of it if he'll be leaving? she asked herself again.

His voice was gruff as he said, "You'd better go."

She mumbled, "I just wanted to apologize."

He nodded, standing perfectly still, his arms straight at his sides.

Her throat tightening, Isobel hurriedly left Neil's office.

If he had called her name, she would have turned back. She would have surrendered to the feelings that seemed right and wrong and everything in-between.

But he didn't, and tears of disappointment and regret filled her eyes.

Chapter Seven

Breathless from exertion, Isobel opened the back door and stepped into the kitchen. Even though it was only 6:45 a.m., her father was sitting at the table reading the morning paper.

"You're up early," he remarked as his gaze swept over her windblown hair, light jacket and workout pants.

She knew he expected an explanation. "I'm going to start cycling regularly again. This morning was the first."

"How many miles did you do?"

"Five. I'll add one each day."

"Pretty soon you'll be getting up at three in the morning to cycle."

"I do have some common sense, Dad. I know I need sleep before I can work."

"What's brought back this sudden interest in bicycling?"

She went to the refrigerator and took out a quart of orange

juice. "No sudden interest. I'd wanted to get back to it. I need the exercise."

"Or maybe you just want to get into better shape for a certain gentleman investigator?"

Was *that* what she was doing? She shook her head. "No, that's not the reason. I've been slacking off."

"You could have fooled me. You usually run around here so fast going from one thing to the other, it makes my head spin."

"I've been slacking off in taking care of myself."

Her father went silent for a few moments, and then said, "Because you've been taking care of me."

"No, Dad, of course not. Life has just gotten busy and I let exercise get lost in the shuffle, that's all."

His brows arched. "And Neil is showing you what you need in your life?"

"Let's just leave Neil out of this, okay?" She poured a glass of juice and quickly downed it.

Her father was still studying her. "You can fool yourself, but you can't fool *me*…about anything. I know you'd rather be living on your own, not having anyone to answer to or do for. Maybe we should consider—"

"Stop telling me what I want, Dad. I'm perfectly happy living here with you, helping you when you need it. Pretty soon that shoulder's going to be better and you'll be driving again."

"Yeah, but I'll still be sixty-eight with creaky bones and arthritis and you'll worry about me. Seriously, Isobel, you should think about getting your own place again."

She could see her dad wasn't going to let this go until she agreed with him. "I'll think about it."

After a few moments her father informed her, "You don't have to worry about supper tonight. A few friends are coming over. We'll order pizza."

"You're going to have fun for a change?" she joked.

"About time, don't you think? You should have some fun, too. Get out more."

A half hour later, Isobel was still considering her conversation with her father when she stepped off the elevator onto the fourth floor of the hospital. She heard a woman's strident voice as she walked down the hall and realized the commotion was at Neil's office door. Mrs. Donaldson, a board member who always held a strong opinion on everything, apparently had her temper up and was pointing her finger at Neil.

Mrs. Donaldson's overstyled ash-blond hair wobbled with her words. "Everyone in this hospital is walking on eggshells around you. They're all afraid to tell you what they think. Well, I'm not. These good people don't deserve the treatment you're giving them. You're even asking *personal* questions. It's none of your business who Peter Wilder is going to marry, or Ella or David. The Wilders practically built this hospital brick by brick. James was a man of integrity and his children are good doctors."

Neil's shoulders were squared and his body tense, his face set on neutral. Isobel knew he was too much of a gentleman to tell the woman what he was thinking. He was too much of a professional to spill his investigation into the hall. But Isobel couldn't let Neil take venom he didn't deserve.

Mrs. Donaldson was pointing her finger again. "Your investigation and your methods are unjust."

Isobel stepped up beside Neil to face Mrs. Donaldson with him. "Mrs. Donaldson, maybe you should think about this more rationally. If something unethical is going on, it should come to light to save Walnut River General…to save James Wilder's legacy. If there *is* wrongdoing, we can't let it destroy the good we do."

Mrs. Donaldson's eyes narrowed and now she targeted Isobel. "You, my dear, are a traitor. The rumors are all over this hospital about your after-hours tête-à-têtes with Mr. Kane."

With that, the woman spun on her heels and headed for the elevator. Several people had come out from their offices and were standing in their doorways listening.

Isobel's eyes suddenly filled with tears. *Were* there rumors about her all over the hospital? *Was* she considered a traitor?

Apparently Neil saw how Mrs. Donaldson's words had affected her because he took her by the elbow and tugged her into his office. After he shut the door, he took her by the shoulders. "You need to forget what that woman said. Someone who searches for the truth is *not* a traitor."

A tear ran down Isobel's cheek and she just let it.

Neil pulled her into his arms, held her for a moment, his chin resting in her curls. "Isobel," he murmured.

As she looked up at him, the few inches of space between them seemed to be too much. His eyes told her he'd missed her and he wanted her. She couldn't deny the missing or the wanting and she lifted her face. He kissed her tears away first and took her lips with a possessiveness that excited her. His tongue didn't wait for an invitation but plunged into her mouth, seducing her into the same rich passion they'd shared before. She blanked out everything but the feel of his hair under her fingertips, his taste, his strength and his desire. Lost in whatever happened whenever they were together, she jumped when there was a sudden knock on the door.

Neil swore. "I'm scheduled for a session with West Mac-Gregor and Richard Green, the lawyer who's filling in for the hospital attorney."

Away from Neil now, letting common sense reign once more, Isobel took a deep breath and pulled herself together fast. She ran a hand through her hair, took a small mirror from her purse and saw the mess her lipstick had become. With a tissue, she eased away the smears as best she could, but she knew she still looked just-kissed.

"Isobel, you're fine. Everything's going to be fine."

How she wished she could believe Neil—but now she felt more like a traitor than she had before…even if there was no basis, even if she was just trying to do what was right.

There was another knock. Neil went to the door and glanced at her. "Ready?"

"As ready as I'm going to be," she assured him.

As he opened the door, she plastered on a bright smile, murmured, "I'm running late. It's good to see you again, West," and then she was practically running down the hall to her office and away from the two men who could probably see she'd been doing more than talking with Neil Kane.

A few hours later, Neil had to admit he was looking for Isobel, not taking a stroll around the hospital to pick up any unusual undercurrents. When he spotted her in a lounge on the second floor talking with a couple, he stopped and observed. He didn't know who the couple were or what they might be discussing. The woman looked distraught, with tears on her cheeks. The man appeared to be upset, too, but was trying to conceal whatever he was feeling to listen to Isobel. Neil could easily see the compassion on Isobel's face. She was leaning into the couple, not backing away. There was no partition that she hid behind. He'd witnessed detachment on social workers' faces, on doctors' faces, so they didn't become too involved with whoever they were helping. Not Isobel. She was right there. That was the thing. She was always right there. Whenever he looked at Isobel, he knew he was missing something important in his life, something he'd done without for far too long. She made him dream again, and he didn't know if that was good or bad.

After a few more minutes she stood, picked up the file folder on the table beside her and left the lounge. She looked startled when she spotted Neil, and glanced at her watch as if she didn't have much time to talk.

"On your way somewhere?" Neil asked.

"Back to my office for a conference call."

Two women brushed by them into the lounge.

"We can talk in the elevator."

"Neil—"

"What? You don't want to be seen walking to the elevator with me?"

"That's not it at all. It's just everything between us is becoming too...too explosive."

Gazing into her dark-brown eyes, wanting to feel her in his arms again, more than ready to take her to his room at the Inn, he knew exactly what she meant. "Come on. The elevator will contain the fireworks."

She shook her head as if she couldn't believe her own stupidity in walking with him and kept pace beside him as he headed for the elevator. Fortunately, he snagged a car that was empty.

As soon as they stepped inside and the doors closed, he assured her, "MacGregor and Green couldn't see us this morning. That frosted window in the door prevents anyone from looking in."

"They didn't have to see us to know what we were doing. One look at my face and hair probably told them everything."

He turned to her and clasped her arm. "What do you want to do?"

She looked troubled and confused and way too vulnerable. "Maybe we need some breathing space."

"Together or apart?"

She just rolled her eyes as the bell in the elevator dinged, announcing their floor.

He pressed the button to keep the door closed. "You want me to stay in my office and keep away from yours. All right, I'll do that. But answer me one question first."

"What?"

She was obviously expecting something personal and that wasn't where he was going. "Who do you think the informant is?"

Her eyes went wide. "The informant? I don't know. I…"

"You said you don't think it's one of the Wilders. What's your gut instinct telling you?"

After she thought about his question, she replied, "The questions you've asked me lead me to think the allegations are about overcharges, or in J. D. Sumner's case, being kept longer than you thought he should be."

Neil didn't confirm or deny that.

"If that's the case, then I think someone in the administrative department is feeding your office the information. I really can't see other personnel knowing as much about it."

"You mean someone in the billing department?"

"Yes, or accounts receivable or even one of the data-entry employees."

"Thanks for narrowing the field," he said wryly.

"I have no clue as to who the person is, Neil. But I think only someone who has access to computer files could be giving you the information."

He nodded, though he didn't say anything. That was the conclusion he'd come to also. He couldn't completely rule out a doctor with a gripe, or one who wanted this takeover to happen. But the kind of information his office had received suggested someone other than a doctor. Maybe more than one person. A doctor being helped by someone in an administrative role?

Isobel hit the open door button on the elevator panel.

"Thanks for your help," Neil told her. "Why don't you head down the hall ahead of me? I'll take my time."

When her gaze met his, he knew what she was thinking. They'd had sex. They'd been as intimate as two people could be. But now they were going to act like strangers because that was easier for her.

And him?

He didn't want to be a stranger to Isobel Suarez, but he couldn't offer her what she obviously deserved—romance, whole-hearted commitment and happily ever after.

He couldn't take his eyes off her as she walked down the hall. He wished he could find the answers he was searching for. He wished he and Isobel could forget the investigation and just live in the moment.

However, he didn't know if living in the moment was enough for him anymore. Maybe he needed to think about the future, too, and whether or not he wanted to live it alone.

An exhausted Isobel walked into her house that night at seven-thirty and was appalled. Cigar smoke stung her nostrils and her lungs as she stepped into the living room. Windbreakers and sweaters were tossed onto the sofa. The remains of a pizza, leftover hot wings and several soda bottles sat on the coffee table and end table. Paper plates were strewn here and there. Men's voices sailed to her from the kitchen. When she headed that way, the smoke was even thicker and she coughed.

Her father had told her he was having friends over, but she'd never expected the place would be totaled.

"A couple more hands, Iz, and we'll be finished."

"If I'm not home by eight-thirty, my wife will be calling every five minutes," Mort Thompson grumbled.

"She worries about you since you had your heart attack," John Suarez insisted.

"She worries too much," Mort murmured.

The men were playing cards around the kitchen table and snacks were tossed here and there and sat beside cups of soda. The smell of burned popcorn hung in the air.

It was going to take hours to clean the place up.

Finding a smile somewhere, she managed to say, "Enjoy your game." To her dad, she said in a low voice, "I'll be down after everyone leaves."

It was her father's turn to play a card but he studied her for a moment and asked, "Are you okay?"

"Tired, Dad. Just tired. I'll take a shower then be back down in a while."

He gave her another careful once-over and then nodded.

Isobel tried not to think or feel as she undressed, took a terrifically long hot shower and towel-dried her hair. She tried to obliterate from her mind the mess downstairs, the work she'd brought home, the moment she'd walked away from Neil, telling herself staying away from him was the best thing to do.

Was it? Didn't she need something else in her life, other than working and taking care of her dad? Didn't she need to be touched and kissed and cared about?

An hour later, dressed in sweats, still wishing she could simply crawl into bed and pull the covers up over her head, she went downstairs and found all the men had left. Her father was transferring snack plates to the kitchen counter, then he attempted to pick up a carrier of soda with his left hand.

When he winced, she hurried over to him. "Dad, you know you have to be careful."

"I never intended for you to have this much of a mess to come home to."

The apology almost made Isobel want to cry. "I know you didn't."

Turning away so he didn't see her emotion, she opened the window over the sink, letting the cool night air push the smoke away.

"I know you hate smoke," he mumbled.

"We'll get it aired out. I can leave the window open overnight."

Wearily he sat down at the table, looked around the room again, and then said determinedly, "This is no life for you—taking care of me, cleaning up after me, doing all the chores you should be doing for your own family."

"*You're* my family."

"Yeah, well, that's probably another reason why you don't have your own family. Besides working so much, I mean."

"Let's not get into this tonight."

"We have to get into it sometime, Iz. Why do you think Jacob stays away? He doesn't want to be saddled with all this." He waved his good arm over the table—the crumbs, napkins and cigar butts.

"You are *not* the reason Jacob stays away. As you said before, he's searching for something."

"Jacob's a good boy at heart, but if he were back here, he'd feel responsible for me, too. Miles away, he doesn't have to worry so much."

In part, Isobel knew that was probably true.

"I should sell the house and look for a small apartment. That way you could get your own place and get on with your life."

"You'd hate a small apartment."

"I'd get used to it. They're building apartments for seniors on the north side of town. I should go look at them."

Her dad took joy in walking around his own yard and re-membering the rosebushes he'd planted for their mother, smelling the lilacs and remembering when the girls had cut them to take to teachers at school. There was the sandbox Jacob had turned into a home for a turtle and the fence they'd all helped paint when they were teenagers. There were years of memories in every room in the house, too.

"Tell me something, Dad, if you hadn't hurt your shoulder, would you even be thinking of selling?"

"Probably not."

"In six weeks, two months, you'll be better. You can't make a rash decision you're going to regret."

"It might get better, it might not. If it's not the shoulder, soon it will be something else. I'm getting older, Iz. What I want won't count for much when I can't do for myself."

She went over to him and crouched down beside his chair. "That's why I want to help you. I'm not here because I have to be. I'm here because I want to be."

"For my sake, not yours."

"Have I complained?" she asked.

"No, but then you wouldn't. That's who you are."

"And I know who *you* are. You want to control your own destiny. I can help you do that."

He patted her shoulder. "You're a good daughter, Isobel." He called her Isobel on important occasions; when she'd learned to ride her first bike, he'd told her, *Now, Isobel, you can go where you want to go.* When she'd earned her driver's license, he'd said, *Driving is a big responsibility, Isobel, don't take advantage of it.* When she graduated from high school and college, he'd insisted, *You're on your way now, Isobel. The whole world's in front of you.*

She wanted the whole world still to be in front of her dad, too. As he'd aged, it had grown smaller. She wanted to keep it as big as she could for him, as long as she could.

"You should never make an important decision when you're tired," she warned him.

"You think something will be different in the morning?"

"I think everything could look different in the morning." She stood and began stacking the dishes in the sink again.

"What can I do to help?"

She knew her father wanted to feel worthwhile, wanted to take some of the burden away from her. "Can you empty the ashtrays? It will get the smell out of here."

"That I can do."

As Isobel watched her dad move around the kitchen and living room, she knew she'd meant everything she'd said to him—but she had to wonder if her life would ever be her own again.

The next morning, when Neil parked in the staff parking lot at the hospital, he noticed Isobel's car rumbling in as he locked his car doors. They hadn't spoken since he'd held the door in the elevator. That seemed like years ago instead of less than twenty-four hours.

The parking space next to his was vacant and although she hesitated a few moments as she drove down the line of slots, she finally turned in beside him. She was wearing a conservative, black two-piece dress today, trimmed in white at the sleeves, lapels and hem. She looked like a million bucks. And she had that unselfconscious style about her that said she didn't know it.

After she pulled her briefcase from her car, she locked her doors.

He went over to her, not knowing if he should. But there'd be no harm in walking her into the hospital. "Good morning."

As he approached her, he could see there were circles under her eyes and she looked pale. But she gave him a forced smile and returned, "Good morning."

He couldn't keep from asking, "Is everything okay?"

She looked so vulnerable for a moment he wanted to gather her into his arms.

"Nothing you'd want to hear about." She started walking toward the building, but he clasped her shoulder and tugged her around.

"Don't make decisions for me, Isobel."

She sighed. "It's just...I didn't sleep well last night. Dad and I had a conversation that bothered me."

"About?"

When she still hesitated, he squeezed her shoulder. "I like your dad and I think he liked me. Is there anything I can do to help?"

"Stop the hands of time," she answered with a sad smile.

"Is your dad not feeling well?"

"It's his emotional state I'm worried about. Last night he told me he should sell the house—"

Her words caught and Neil could see how upset she was. He hugged her. He couldn't help it. At first she was stiff in his arms, but then she seemed to need the contact, too. Finally she looked up at him and, oh, how he wanted to kiss her. But they were standing in the public parking lot and he knew how she'd feel about that after it was over, especially if there were witnesses.

He glanced up at the row of hospital rooms that overlooked the lot.

She realized what he was thinking and quickly pulled away from him.

"Do you know what I think?" he asked.

"I'm afraid to ask," she murmured.

"I think we both need to get away."

She sighed heavily. "That's the whole point, Neil. I can't. I'm taking care of my dad."

"Don't tell me you can't get away for a weekend."

"Away where?"

"You said you were working on an auction for the senior center and you needed donations. How would you like something really great?"

"What kind of great?" she asked warily.

"Maybe an antique?"

"And you know someone who will be willing to donate an antique?"

"I might. Come away with me this weekend and we'll find out."

He could see the thoughts flipping through her mind.

"Look, I know what you're thinking. But this weekend can be whatever you want it to be. My parents live about two hours north. I haven't seen them for a few months and when I called Mom on Sunday to wish her a happy Mother's Day, she dropped a big hint that, though she liked the flowers I sent her, she'd like a visit from me even more. Antique shops are pretty common in their area. I happen to know the owner of one fairly well. You can pick out what you want, and I'll donate the antique. We can stay at an inn…in separate rooms, of course."

Isobel didn't say no right away and that was a great sign. But she did study him carefully. He could feel her gaze as if it were a touch on his eyes, on his mouth and back to his eyes again.

"Why are you doing this?" she wanted to know.

"I'm doing it because we both need a respite. I'm tired of feeling as if I'm in a fishbowl every time I talk to you. Besides that, I need perspective on the investigation and maybe you need perspective on what's going on with your dad."

"No *maybe* about it," she murmured.

He knew he couldn't push Isobel into this. It had to be a free decision on her part.

"I could ask Debbie if she'd mind if Dad stayed over with her this weekend."

"There's another solution," Neil offered. "Maybe Chad could just stay with your dad. He could keep a watchful eye on him, but your father wouldn't feel as if he's being coddled."

Isobel looked uncertain.

"I know, you probably need time to think about all this. Have dinner with me tonight. If you decide you want to do it, we can stop at your sister's and you can ask."

"Dad might not be all bent out of shape about it if Chad stayed with him," she agreed. "But I won't have time for a long dinner—"

"We can stop for fast food if you want. I don't care."

"The Chinese Kitchen is fast," she offered, finally accepting his invitation.

"The Chinese Kitchen it is." He suddenly realized that no matter what happened today, he'd have Isobel to look forward to this evening.

That thought could keep him smiling through anything.

Chapter Eight

Isobel had just finished with a patient one of the E.R. docs had referred to her when Simone Gardner snagged her arm. "Got a minute?" the pretty brunette E.R. nurse asked.

Isobel and Simone had become good friends over the past six months—good enough friends to confide in each other about their lives and pasts. "I always have a minute for you. I've been meaning to call you. How are you feeling?"

Simone was three months pregnant and glowing with the promise of motherhood. Some of that glow might also be due to her upcoming wedding to medic Mike O'Rourke. A one-night stand had led to what they'd hoped would be a lifetime of happiness.

Isobel thought of Neil, felt a pang of envy, and then quickly brushed it away. She was happy for her friend. That one-night stand had turned out well for her. Isobel considered the upcoming weekend, what might or might not happen. *Her* circumstances were very different. Neil didn't even live in Walnut River.

"I'm feeling good," Simone responded, answering her question. "I've had some morning sickness but it seems to be getting better now."

"How are the plans for the wedding?"

"They're going fine. I invited my mother."

Simone and her mother had long had a difficult relationship. "How do you feel about that?"

"I'm okay with it. She's attending the date-rape support group you recommended. I've noticed an improvement in her outlook since she's going to the group. She actually seems pleased to know that my future looks bright and happy. She's even a little bit excited about the wedding. It's going to be small," Simone went on. "But I'd like you to be my maid of honor. Will you? You don't need a special dress. I'm wearing a white suit."

"You've set the date?"

"The last Saturday in May in Mike's parents' backyard. Are you free?"

Would Neil still be around at the end of May? Probably not. "I'll be there. Just let me know what time."

Simone nodded and then leaned a bit closer. "I hear you're on a first-name basis with that investigator. What goes with that?"

Isobel didn't know what to say. She didn't want to lie to her friend, and she knew Simone would keep whatever she said in confidence. But what was there to say?

"Uh-oh, don't tell me the rumors are true," Simone surmised, probably correctly.

"What rumors?"

Simone hesitated.

Isobel knew her friend was not one to gossip. "I need to know, Simone."

Her friend finally revealed, "You've been seen outside the hospital with Neil Kane, at The Crab Shack, at the Walnut River Inn. Are you involved with him?"

Again, Isobel wasn't sure how to respond. So she simply said, "I like him."

Simone studied her more closely. "Oh, Isobel."

"What?"

"I can see it in your eyes. You've fallen for him."

In a quiet voice, she answered, "Maybe I have."

"Is there a future in this?"

"How *can* there be when he'll be going back to Boston when he's finished here?"

"Are you going to be with him while he's here?"

Simone knew all about falling in love against her will. Sometimes the heart made the most important decisions. Isobel knew she could trust her friend. "I'm going away with him this weekend. We're going to pick up an antique for the senior citizen auction."

There was a knowing look in Simone's eyes.

"We're going to have separate rooms," Isobel insisted.

"That doesn't mean you'll *stay* in separate rooms."

Just thinking about that possibility, Isobel's heart raced. "I'm not sure what I'm going to do. I do know that for once in my life, I'm not going to plan the future. I might even live in the moment. That will be a first."

"And damn the consequences?" Simone asked.

"And damn the consequences. Being with Neil for more than a snatched hour here and there might show me I don't care about him the way I think I do. This could be an eye-opening experience."

Simone clasped Isobel's arm. "I don't have any advice to give. Look what happened to me." She patted her tummy, which wasn't yet round. "But I can tell you I'm happier than I've ever been and that's all because of Mike."

Isobel gave her friend a hug. "I'm looking forward to your wedding."

"You can bring a guest," Simone suggested slyly.

"I'm not planning the future, remember?"

"Right."

A voice on the loudspeaker paged Simone.

"Break's over. I've got to scoot. I know you do, too." Before she hurried away, Simone suggested, "If you need someone to talk to when you get back, call me."

Isobel nodded, grateful Simone was her friend. Maybe when she returned to Walnut River, she wouldn't feel as confused as she did right now.

"So Cyrus is visiting with Dad?" Debbie asked Neil and Isobel as she brought the two of them sodas.

Neil was sitting on the sofa next to Isobel, his arm and leg lodged next to hers. He hadn't even kissed her yet tonight. In some ways, he felt like a teenager again, trying to read his date's cues.

"Cyrus was there when I got home," Isobel explained. "He said he was taking Dad to Burger King for supper. By the time I'd changed, they'd gone."

"Good for Cyrus. I'm grateful he's getting Dad out of the house."

"Actually your dad is why I'm here," Neil explained. "I want Isobel to go with me this weekend to my hometown.

I think I can finagle a couple of antiques for the senior center's auction."

"That would be great," Debbie said enthusiastically. "Do you want Dad to come over here?"

Isobel jumped in now. "I don't know how he'll feel about that, if he'll think we're taking care of him again. But Neil had a good idea. How do you think Chad would feel about staying with Dad Saturday and Sunday, instead of Dad coming over here?"

Debbie thought about it. "That might work. Chad's responsible enough. But he has to feel comfortable with doing it." She yelled, "Hey, Chad! Come here a minute, will you?"

The teenager emerged from his room in an oversize T-shirt and torn jeans. When he saw Neil, he grinned. "Did you come over for another game?"

"Not this time. Your aunt has a favor to ask."

Chad looked at Isobel. "What's up?"

She told him.

"So you want me to make sure Gramps eats and doesn't fall or anything?"

"Only if you're comfortable with staying," Isobel assured him.

"It will be cool. He can get out all those old photograph albums and tell me stories, and we can play cards. I know I might have to watch the History Channel with him, but I've got my iPod."

"You really don't mind?" Isobel asked.

"Nope. Stephanie's out of town this weekend so I'm high and dry."

"Except for that paper that's due," his mother reminded him.

"I'm going to finish that up tonight."

Apparently Stephanie was Chad's girlfriend. Neil could see the teenager really wouldn't mind looking after his grandfather.

Isobel assured Chad, "I have casseroles in the freezer I can take out before we leave for Saturday night and Sunday. There should be enough of everything else in the refrigerator—eggs, deli meat for the rest of the meals."

"We can always order pizza," Chad joked. "While you and Mom talk about what we're going to eat and all…" He cast a look at Neil. "Can I talk to you for a minute?"

Neil was surprised at the request. "Sure." Chad motioned to him. "Come back to my room. I want to show you something."

Still puzzled, Neil followed Chad to his bedroom. It was decorated like any teenage boy's bedroom with a poster of Carrie Underwood on one wall, an enlarged photo of David Ortiz at bat on the other. A computer sat on a small hutch.

"What did you want to show me?" Neil asked.

"Nothing really. I wanted to ask you something."

"About?"

"Well, Mom said you were married once."

"Yes, I was." He wondered if this was about Chad's dad and the divorce.

"But you're single now, right?"

"Sure am."

"And you like Aunt Iz?" Chad raised his brows.

There was no use denying it. "Yes, I do."

"Do you date a lot?"

"Not so much. I'm working most of the time."

"But you *do* date?"

"I do."

"See, I'm dating this girl," Chad explained.

"Stephanie."

"Yeah, and she's really hot. She's nice, too, and I like her a lot."

"So what's the problem?"

"I want to buy a car. Mom says she won't get me one and she won't let Dad get me one. But if I save up on my own and find one, she won't say I can't buy it. So I want to work all summer and save the money."

"That sounds like a plan."

"It *was* a plan until Steph asked me to go to the beach with her and her family for the month of July. They rent a house and her relatives come and go."

"So if you go with her for the month of July, you won't save nearly as much money."

"Right. But if I stay here and work, she might break up with me."

"How much does she mean to you?"

Chad looked down at his sneakers and rubbed his toe against the carpet. "A whole lot. She's the kind of girl I could see marrying some day. You know what I mean?"

"Can you live without the car?"

"I really want wheels."

"It's not an easy decision, Chad, but you're going to have to decide what's more important to you and live with whatever you decide."

"I want to work it so I can do both."

Neil chuckled. "Don't we all! But life rarely gives us everything we want. If Stephanie likes you as much as you like her, maybe she'll live without you for the month, and then get back together with you when she returns."

"Or, she could meet some surfer dude down there and I'd be toast."

"That's the chance you'd have to take."

Chad frowned. "I thought you'd have some answers."

Neil almost laughed out loud but he didn't because he was afraid Chad would misunderstand. "If you think you're going to find the answers as you get older, I can tell you you'll find some of them, but mostly you'll just find out what means the most to you."

"And that's what I have to figure out? Whether Stephanie's more important than the car?"

"Or whether trusting her is as important as the car."

"That's a different take on it," Chad mumbled. After a few seconds of silence, he shook his head and grinned ruefully. "And here I thought guys your age knew what to do about women."

"Not a chance. Even the ones who pretend to know what they're doing don't."

Chad gave him a sideways glance. "So what about you and Aunt Iz? Is something really happening?"

Neil was tempted to say, "After this weekend I'll let you know," but he knew better. He also knew after this weekend things could even be more complicated than they were now, especially if he took Isobel to his parents' home. "I don't discuss the women in my life. That's something I *have* learned in forty-two years."

Ten minutes later, after Chad showed him the iPod his father had gotten for him—another toy to make up for not being with him—Neil went back to the living room. All he wanted to do was take Isobel back to the Inn and spend the night with her. But he knew that likely wouldn't happen tonight. So instead, he waited until she'd ironed out every detail of Chad staying with her dad and then they left.

At the car, he opened the door for her. She slid inside and then looked up at him. He was broadsided by that look, by the beauty in Isobel that she couldn't herself see. Tonight she was dressed in a red-checkered blouse and navy slacks. Large red hoops swung from her ears. They both seemed lost in the moment because neither of them moved and neither of them spoke.

Suddenly he realized Isobel's sister was probably watching from a window, maybe even Chad, too. "Do you know how much I've wanted to kiss you all night?"

"No," she said with a shy smile.

"Will you come back to the Inn with me?"

"I don't think that's a good idea."

His heart sank. Maybe this weekend was going to be merely about antiques.

But Isobel hurried on. "I really don't want to be the butt of gossip."

He understood that the rumors really bothered her. But Isobel was always used to being in the right place at the right time and doing the right thing. Being with him wasn't wrong, but clearly it didn't seem right, either.

He closed her door none too gently, rounded the front of the car, and climbed into the driver's seat. After he did, she surprised him and leaned over, kissing him softly on the lips. She was there and then she was gone and he wanted a hell of a lot more.

"What was that for?" he asked, his voice husky as he backed out of her sister's driveway.

"For being so patient and letting me and Debbie iron out everything. What did Chad want to show you?"

"He showed me his iPod, but what he really wanted was to ask my advice on a girl problem. For some reason he thought I'd have the answer."

"And did you?"

"No, I just gave him food for thought. He's only trying to figure out what will make him happy."

"Good luck to him. At thirty-five, I'm still not sure," Isobel remarked.

Neil knew exactly what she meant.

They'd almost reached her dad's house when she said, "Cyrus's car is still parked in front. Don't stop. Go down to the next block and make a left turn."

"Where are we going?"

"You'll see." She directed him to make another left and he turned onto the gravel alley that stretched in back of the houses.

"There's a parking space next to Dad's garage. Pull in there and cut the lights."

After he did as she directed, he had to laugh. "I feel like a teenager again doing something illicit," he said with a smile.

"Doesn't that make it all the more fun?"

He couldn't see her in the pitch-blackness but he could hear the excited amusement in her voice. After he unfastened his seat belt, he took her into his arms, then he kissed her as he'd been wanting to kiss her all night. His hands were in her soft curls but his tongue was teasing her lips apart. His body was thrumming with all the restrained desire he'd been keeping in check.

She reached for him in the same hungry way, her fingers digging into his shoulders, her body straining toward his, her soft sounds of pleasure giving him all the permission he needed to take the kiss deeper, make it hotter and wetter. The steering wheel was in his way and the last thing he wanted to do was dig his elbow into the horn.

He broke away from her and leaned his forehead against hers. "Let's move into the backseat. We'll have more room."

She stilled. "Neil, I don't know if I want to—"

"I just want to hold you without wrecking the GPS or alerting the whole neighborhood we're here by hitting the horn."

After a long moment, she whispered, "Okay."

After they'd moved to the backseat, he gathered her into his arms for a long hug. He kissed her temple and ran his hand through her hair. "This isn't about me wanting sex again. It's about me wanting *you*."

She turned her head into his neck and her breath was warm against his skin when she said, "I'm scared, Neil. We could be over in a blink of an eye."

"Do you want to go in?" He wasn't going to coax her into something she wasn't sure about, no matter how much his body tried to persuade him otherwise.

"Can we just stay here like this for a little while?"

Holding her and breathing her in was better than leaving her at her door. It was better than going back to that lonely bed at the Inn…better than erotic dreams that left him sweating and needing, with his arms empty.

"I'll hold you for as long as you want me to." Tonight, Isobel needed him in just this way. His needs would just have to be put on hold until she decided whether or not an affair with him would be worth the heartache.

Seizing the moment didn't seem so simple anymore.

As Neil drove two hours northeast to the town of Cranshaw on Saturday, Isobel couldn't believe how patient he'd been with her this week. She remembered how he'd held her without pushing for more on Wednesday night, how he'd kissed her, restraining himself from letting desire get out of control. Thursday night she'd been on call and had to handle a readmission. Last night…

They'd parked by her dad's garage again and Neil had sensed how much she'd needed to cuddle with him again in the silence.

It was scary sometimes how much he understood her. How was that possible in such a short time?

They didn't talk as they drove, just listened to music and held hands now and then across the middle of the car.

When they reached the outskirts of Cranshaw, she saw Neil stiffen, his hands becoming tighter on the wheel. How hard was this trip to his parents going to be?

"Your mom knows we're coming?"

"Yes, she does. Believe me, I'd never surprise them with an unexpected visit."

"Why not?"

"My parents aren't like your dad, Isobel. They're not all-embracing. Mom wants to be, but Dad is too…unrelenting. She'll pull out all the stops tonight, though, so be prepared."

"Pull out all the stops?"

"White linen tablecloth, candles, good silver, her mother's china."

"Does she do that for you?"

"Sometimes. She feels she's making my homecoming special that way. But tonight, she's doing it because I'm bringing a guest." As they drove through the center of town, they passed a huge brick-and-stone building with marble steps.

"The courthouse?" she asked.

"Yep. Dad worked there most of his life. I was really surprised when he retired two years ago. But he's writing a book on sentencing and the prison system. That's been keeping him busy."

The square in Cranshaw was the busiest intersection. Two streets later, Neil took a left turn, then a right. There was a row of shops, each painted a different color—yellow, royal blue, red and one white one. Antiques and More was the red structure which stood on the end. The other businesses housed a women's boutique, a flower shop and an optician.

All had similar window boxes filled with flowers and dark wood doors that stood open on the warm afternoon.

"The proprietors of all four shops decided they wanted to stand out. Even with the strip mall at the south side of town and a major mall on the north, these specialty shops do a good business. Come on, I'll introduce you to Mrs. Springer. She was my high-school math teacher."

Neil didn't give Isobel time to comment. He just hopped out of the car and came around to her door.

When she took his hand to climb out of the car, she asked, "Is Mrs. Springer going to tell me some good stories about you?"

"Not if I can help it."

A bell over the door jingled as Neil and Isobel went inside the shop. There were old photographs on the walls, furniture here and there, china and collectibles in cases. The woman at the cashier's desk was tall and thin, with gray hair piled into curls on the top of her head. She wore bright pink lipstick and a smock over her knit shirt and jeans.

When she saw Neil, she hurried toward him and gave him a big hug. "How are you doing, Neil? It's so good to see you. What's it been? Two, three years?"

"About that. It's good to see you, too, Mrs. Springer. I'd like to introduce you to Isobel Suarez. She's the woman I told you about who's collecting items for the senior citizens' auction in Walnut River."

"How many times do I have to tell you it's Helen. You're out of school now, Neil…been out a long time." She vigorously shook Isobel's hand. "It's good to meet you."

"Neil just told me you were his math teacher."

"That I was. He was one of my most promising students. He could have been a mathematician—clearheaded, fast-thinking, calculated quicker in his head than anyone could on the calculator."

Isobel quirked her eyebrows at Neil. "A hidden talent you haven't told me about?"

"One of many," he joked. "Actually what I do isn't that different from mathematics. I add up the information, subtract whatever is irrelevant and figure out the solution."

"Your dad was right, you know. You would have made a good lawyer," Mrs. Springer commented.

Neil went silent.

Mrs. Springer, sensing she'd said the wrong thing, clasped Neil's arm. "But I understand you had to take your own road. It's just hard for a lot of parents who have their minds made up about what their children should be to accept something different."

Avoiding the topic altogether, Neil motioned to the merchandise in the shop. "So do you think you can help us? I'm searching for a couple of pieces I can buy and donate to the auction."

"Price range?" Helen asked.

"About five hundred total."

"Neil!" Isobel was shocked. "You don't have to donate that much. I never dreamed—"

When Neil hung his arm around Isobel's shoulders, she felt as if she belonged there, next to him, by his side. "Let me do this, Isobel. It's a worthy cause and I'll be able to see directly where it's going."

Her heart tripped. "You think you'll be coming back to visit after the investigation?"

Gazing down at her, he nodded. "I'd say that's a likely possibility."

Helen was watching them, taking it all in. She motioned to

them. "Come into the back room with me. I have a couple of pieces I just touched up. You'll want something useful that even someone who doesn't know antiques might buy. I have a Chippendale chair that's just been reupholstered and a nice claw-foot side table. If you have enough time, I can show you some pieces I've been saving for the summer tourist rush—Roseville pottery."

"Now *that* I could fit in my car. We have plenty of time, Helen." In Isobel's ear, he whispered, "We don't want to arrive at my parents' house any sooner than we have to."

Isobel hadn't been particularly nervous before, but now…

Neil's parents certainly wouldn't be ogres, but the way he was describing his dad, she suspected tonight could be uncomfortable at the least, confrontational at the worst, and maybe not even friendly.

What had she gotten herself into?

Chapter Nine

"My father inherited the house from his father," Neil explained as he drove up a treelined drive.

If a house could impress Isobel, the Kanes' house would. Stone and brick, it sat atop a hill with a long drive leading up to it. Surrounded by oaks, maples, spruce and pine, the three-story dwelling was stately and elegant, just like the property.

He added, "The Kanes helped settle Cranshaw and they've always been instrumental in running the town. My grandfather, who was also once a criminal defense attorney, became mayor after he retired."

"So he was around when you were growing up?"

"He was. We lived on the other side of town, and I used to ride my bike over. I could spend hours in his library. He died when I was in college. When my parents moved in, I chose a room on the third floor. It's like being at the top of the world up there."

She peered at the third-floor gables. "I can see why. It's a beautiful house."

"My parents finally seemed happier after they moved here. Maybe because there weren't any reminders of Garrett."

This was the first Neil had mentioned his brother since that one reference to him dying. "Were *you* happier?"

His answer was quick in coming. "I had moved on. But happier? No."

She could see now that his brother's death had affected him deeply.

They parked in front of a three-car garage that was attached to the house by a breezeway. Instead of going to the front door, Neil led Isobel to the breezeway door and they stepped inside.

She could see the area was sort of like her dad's glassed-in porch. The furniture was verdigris with huge soft cushions. The tables were metal and glass, and the ceramic-tile floor was the same rust shade as the cushions. A small gas-burning stove filled one corner.

"This is lovely," Isobel remarked, trying to take it all in. The backyard was immense.

"I spent a lot of time out here when I came home from college."

Because he'd still felt separated from his parents? Choosing a room on the third floor set him apart from them. Had he stayed removed because of guilt? He'd told her that when Garrett had been born, he'd felt displaced. After his brother had died, he'd felt responsible. At a time when a boy needed his parents most, she had the feeling a wall of pain had blocked Neil from his. She suddenly realized that she not only recognized Neil's pain, but actually *felt* it. She hurt for him; she hurt with him. And now she knew why.

She loved him.

She didn't know when or how it had happened. But she was head over heels. He'd become integral to her life, and in such a short time. The reality of love was so huge, the rush of emotion so great, it frightened her.

Without thinking twice, she slipped her hand into his.

The doors of the house flew open and Neil's mother— at least Isobel assumed she was Neil's mother—stood there grinning at them. In her mid-sixties, Alice Kane was still a beautiful woman. Her frosted-blond wavy hair was styled attractively around her face. She was wearing a pale-peach sweater, shirt and knit slacks. Her eyes were the same golden brown as Neil's. Although she appeared glad to see him, she didn't run forward and embrace him, nor did he embrace her.

Isobel keenly felt the absence of that hug.

When Neil released Isobel's hand and hung his arm around her shoulders, he said, "Mom, I'd like you to meet Isobel Suarez. Isobel, this is my mother, Alice Kane."

Isobel extended her hand. "It's nice to meet you, Mrs. Kane."

"Call me Alice," the older woman insisted. She stepped back and motioned them into the kitchen. "Come on in." She said to Neil, "I baked your favorite oatmeal cookies." As he passed her, she laid her hand on his shoulder.

Isobel could feel that these two wanted to be close, yet something was standing in their way. The judge, maybe?

"I have trays set up in the parlor," Alice hurried on. "We have coffee, tea, hot chocolate, whatever you want."

Isobel glanced around the bright kitchen with its birch cupboards, stainless-steel appliances and an island in the center. A bright-red table and chairs sat under a flowered chandelier, and Isobel could peek into the large dining room beyond. The teakettle simmered on the stove and the aroma of fresh coffee floated through the air. Cookies were laid out on a beautiful glass tray covered with plastic wrap.

"You don't have to carry everything into the parlor. We can just sit at the table," Neil suggested.

"Oh, but your father said he'd prefer—"

An older man who Isobel guessed was in his late sixties entered the kitchen then. He was tall, with glasses and completely gray hair. He was wearing an oxford-cloth shirt and casual slacks and loafers. His cheekbones were higher than Neil's, his jaw a little less defined, but she could see the resemblance.

"What do I prefer?" he asked with a tight smile and a nod toward Neil and Isobel.

Awkwardness filled the kitchen but Neil replied easily. "I told Mom she didn't have to go to all the trouble of setting up the parlor. We're fine at the table."

Already Isobel felt the tight wire of tension pull between the two men. "That's fine," Neil's father agreed, not making it an issue. "Introduce me to your…friend."

Neil made the introductions while his mother bustled about, putting the cookies on the table, gathering cups and saucers and goblets.

"My wife tells me you're a social worker, Isobel," the judge remarked. "You must see as much dirty family laundry as I did when I was on the bench."

"I get involved in family dynamics," she admitted. "Fortunately, I feel I can make a difference. I imagine it was frustrating for you to see the results of family situations gone wrong."

"That's perceptive of you," he said, studying her more closely, waiting for his wife to pour his coffee.

Neil remained silent. Still, his father targeted him next. "We've heard all about the Northeastern HealthCare takeover attempt in Walnut River. We're afraid they might try here next. Are you investigating what they're trying to do?" he asked his son.

"No, I'm not."

"And of course you can't say more about it."

"No, I can't."

The judge crossed his arms over his chest. "How soon will you be returning to Boston?"

"I'm not sure, a week or two."

The judge assessed Neil's neutral expression, then gave his son a slight smile that didn't carry much warmth. "Have you thought about what I advised the last time you were home—running for office? Even though you're not a lawyer, with the experience you've gotten, you could make a place for yourself in the State House, maybe even run for governor someday."

"I told you before, Dad, getting involved in politics is the last thing I'd ever consider," Neil said calmly as if the calmness was hard to come by.

"You're really satisfied with what you're doing?"

"Let's not get into this now, Dad, okay? Isobel and I just dropped by for a friendly visit."

As if his mother heard the restrained impatience in Neil's tone, she rushed in. "Did you find any antiques at Mrs. Springer's?"

"We did. Isobel thinks they'll go over well at the auction."

"Auction?" his father asked.

"It's a charity auction at the senior citizens' center in

Walnut River. Neil kindly bought a few items at Mrs. Springer's and is donating them." Isobel flashed a smile at Neil's father.

"Oh, he did?" Neil's father gave his son a long look and then appraised *her* carefully. His perusal was making her uncomfortable so she filled in the silence.

"Mrs. Springer even donated a small table we could fit in the back of the car. I might end up being auctioneer unless we can find someone more experienced. I'll be familiar with each item, but I've never done an auction."

"I helped with a silent auction last year," Alice said cheerily. She began telling Isobel about the charity benefit.

As Isobel listened, she wondered if this family had experienced any truly happy moments since Garrett had died. There was a chasm between Neil and his father that his mother obviously tried to fill, yet she couldn't, because she felt torn between the two of them.

Isobel felt Judge Kane's constant regard as Neil's mom gave her a tour of her gardens and they talked about flowers and landscaping. She felt his gaze on her often throughout dinner.

Afterward as dusk began to fall, Neil pulled her outside onto the patio. She supposed he wanted to give both of them a break.

The night air was cool and Neil stood close enough that she could feel his body heat. "Do you want to go to the inn now? We don't have to stay."

"You haven't seen your parents in a while, Neil. Don't you want to spend some time with them?"

"You've gotten a taste of what it's like being with my parents. I don't want you to feel uncomfortable. This was a bad idea. I don't know what I thought I'd accomplish."

"Did you want *them* to meet *me,* or *me* to meet *them?*"

He didn't pretend not to know what she meant. Had he brought her here so his parents might approve of her? Or had he brought her here so she could get a peek into his life, what it had been and what it was now.

"I'm not sure. Every time I come home I think things might be different. They never are."

"Your mom is sweet. She tries to make up for the tension between you and your dad."

"If it weren't for Mom, I wouldn't come home."

Suddenly the patio lights went on. They lit the perimeter of the flagstone and dispelled the approaching shadows. The French door that separated the dining room from the patio opened and Judge Kane stepped outside. It was obvious he noticed how close Neil and Isobel were standing.

He wore a light jacket and he brought Isobel's sweater to her. She'd left it in the kitchen. "I thought you might need this."

Neil silently took it from his father and held it while Isobel inserted first one arm and then the other. "Thank you," she told the older man, looking for signs of softening in his face. There weren't any.

He addressed Neil. "I'd like to talk to Isobel for a few minutes. Alone."

"Why is that necessary?" Neil countered, on the defensive, ready to protect her.

Isobel wanted to know what the judge was thinking and to get a glimpse behind the stoic facade he wore. "It's all right, Neil."

"You're sure?" It was his investigator's voice that wanted the truth.

"I'm sure. I'd like to get to know your dad better."

"I'll be in the living room," he told her as he went inside. She knew if she needed him, all she had to do was call.

A slight breeze ruffled the leaves on the decades-old trees and blew Isobel's hair across her cheek. She swept it away and just waited.

"Let's get to the bottom line," the judge decided. "Are you and my son serious?"

"Maybe you should be asking *him* that," she responded softly.

He frowned. "I didn't come out here to spar with you."

"Why *did* you come out here?"

He looked a little surprised that she was questioning him. "I want to know what Neil's getting himself into. It's been a long time since he brought a woman here."

"Exactly how long has it been?" she asked.

As if debating whether he wanted to answer her or not, he took a few moments, then he replied, "He hasn't brought anyone here since his divorce."

Could Neil really be serious about her? Did they have a chance to be together beyond his investigation?

Before she could even answer those questions in her mind, the judge warned, "Don't think you're going to get your hands on his money. After one failed marriage, I'm sure he'd ask for a prenuptial agreement."

"I didn't know Neil had any money," she blurted out honestly.

The judge motioned to the house and the surroundings. "When you saw this, you knew. I'm sure Neil indicated the lifestyle he grew up with."

"Your property and standard of living has nothing to do with Neil now."

"He'll inherit someday. A smart woman—and you strike me as a smart woman—will consider that."

Up until now, Isobel had tried to remain polite. After all, these were Neil's parents and, truth be told, she wanted them to like her. But the judge already had a preconceived notion of who she was. So maybe she needed to do some plain speaking to get her point across.

She looked him straight in the eye. "Money can't buy happiness. If I wanted proof of that, I can look at you and your wife and know it."

He blustered. "Who do you think—?"

She held up her hand to stop him. "I know about loss. My mother died four years ago. Not a day goes by that I don't miss her. No amount of money will bring her back. I suspect that's what you feel about the son you lost. Neil told me there's distance between you two, and that's what I can't understand. You lost one son, but you still have Neil. You should be proud you raised such a wonderful man and you should be doing everything in your power not to lose him, too!"

Silence stretched long between them until the judge decided, "This isn't any of your business."

"You made it my business when you came out here to question me."

After he studied her for a few tense moments, he looked into the darkness and the trees in the backyard. "Neil and I haven't been close since before Garrett died."

"Is that because Garrett was your favorite?"

When the judge's gaze found hers, she knew she was right.

"Maybe he was after he was born, but I was always proud of Neil. I had great expectations for him. He could have been anything he'd chosen to be. If he didn't want to go into law, he could have become a doctor, a physicist, absolutely anything. But he has no ambition. You heard what he said about going into politics."

She leaned forward, interested in how Neil's father

thought. "Why do you believe ambition has to be lofty? Neil became a police officer so he could catch the bad guys. Now he holds a trusted position in the Attorney General's Office. Why isn't it enough for you that he cares about what he does, that he thinks he can right wrongs his way?"

Neil's dad fell into silence again. Finally, he asked, "That's the way he sees it?"

"Yes, that's the way he sees it. As a judge, you see the results of a situation. Neil takes an active part in finding out the truth, making sure the right person gets blamed, which doesn't always happen in the legal system."

When Neil's father didn't respond, Isobel wondered if maybe she should leave him and go inside.

His voice was somewhat less arrogant when he concluded, "You and my son have more than a…surface relationship."

She knew what those code words meant. The judge thought they were sleeping together and that's what had brought them together. Maybe their attraction had brought them together, but she and Neil communicated on lots of other levels, too. "Yes, we do."

"I don't meet many young women who say what's on their mind in such a thoughtful manner," he admitted a bit awkwardly.

"I handle sticky situations a lot, so I've had practice."

The judge gave a light chuckle. "You're a match for Neil. I can see that. He needs a strong woman. He has a stubborn streak that I'm sure he didn't inherit from me." There was some slight amusement in Neil's dad's words and she wondered what would happen if he and his son had an honest and heartfelt conversation.

The subtle relaxation of tension between them led Isobel to say, "I think you and Neil are more alike than you realize."

"But we don't want to admit it?"

With her cards on the table as well as his, she could afford to be diplomatic, "Something like that."

"I think I just saw Neil's shadow pass by the French doors. We'd better assure him I haven't upset you to the point of tears."

"You haven't upset me, Judge," she assured him.

He opened the door. "Good, because I think I'd like to have more conversations with you in the future."

Neil was standing inside, and he studied her closely. "Everything okay?"

To Neil's surprise, the judge patted his shoulder. "If she can hold her own with me, she can hold her own with anyone." He shrugged out of his jacket. "I'm going to find your mother and see if I can rustle up another piece of that apple pie. If you're interested," he pointed his thumb at the kitchen, "I'll be in there."

After his dad left the room, Neil took Isobel by the shoulders. "I hope he didn't insult you. He has a way—"

"He didn't. Actually I think your dad and I understand each other."

Neil finally broke into a smile. "The same way *your* dad and I understand each other?"

"Precisely."

He shook his head. "You'll have to tell me about it. Do you want a piece of pie?"

She didn't, but she could nibble while Neil and his father took a few tenuous steps toward each other. "I'll have a cup of tea. You have a piece of pie and we'll see if we can't have some conversation that doesn't put everyone on edge."

"That'll be the day." Neil brought her into his chest for a tight hug and a quick but deep kiss. When they broke apart, he said, "We have separate rooms at the inn and that's the way it will stay if you want it that way. But I—"

Neil's cell phone rang. After he fished it out of his pocket, he checked the caller ID. "It's my office. I need to take this."

Apparently Neil's office never shut down and he was always on call. She wished their kiss had been longer, deeper, more intimate. Tonight…

She still hadn't made up her mind about tonight. She reached up and stroked his jaw. "I'll save you a piece of pie," she assured him, and went to the kitchen, considering the consequences of joining Neil in his room tonight…considering her regrets if she didn't.

Neil's phone call had troubled him, Isobel could tell. He'd acted as if it hadn't. He'd eaten his piece of pie, complimented his mother on it again, and asked his dad how his book was going. But underneath it all, she could see in his eyes when he looked at her that the call had bothered him.

He'd been so careful with her as they'd checked in at the Victorian inn where he'd reserved their rooms. He'd kissed her good-night at her door—the other room on their floor was unoccupied—with more restraint than she'd ever felt him use. It hadn't been what she'd expected at all. She'd expected to be swept away. She'd expected him to kiss her senseless until there was no decision to make. But he hadn't. He'd told her he'd see her in the morning and went into his room, next to hers.

Isobel changed into her nightgown. She attempted to read and didn't absorb any of the words on the page. She tried to sleep but thoughts of Neil and what they could be doing together kept her awake. Then there were the sounds from his room, the creak of the floorboards, first on one side of the room and then the other, the hum of the small printer he carried with his computer that told her he might be working, the sound of his door opening as he went into the bathroom, ran the shower, and then returned once more to his bedroom.

Maybe if she took a shower she'd be able to sleep, maybe it would relax her. Twenty minutes later, Isobel had showered, too, and dried her hair. It was a soft mass of wild curls all over her head. After she slipped on her nightgown once more, she studied her face in the mirror.

What do you really want? she asked herself.

That answer was easy—another night with Neil, a whole night with Neil, maybe every night with Neil until he left Walnut River. Sure, she could try to keep her heart safe. She could pretend the love she felt for him would go away after he was gone. She could deny the desire that right now made her feel more alive than she'd ever felt before.

Or...

She could take the risk of finding out if he wanted her as much as she wanted him.

Sliding into the satin mules that matched her gown—the slippers, gown and robe had been a set Debbie had given her last Christmas—she left the robe hanging on the bathroom door. She hesitated in the hall outside Neil's room. Was she being altogether foolish?

There was only one way to find out. She knocked.

When Neil answered his door, his face was more stoic than she'd ever seen it. He looked down over the pale-green, satin nightgown, his gaze lingering on her breasts, on the curve of her hips, before returning to her face. "Do you need something?"

His voice was gravelly and she hoped that was because she was affecting him the way he was affecting her. He wore navy flannel jogging shorts and a drawstring dangled tantalizingly at his navel. She was going to hyperventilate if she didn't get this over with and find out if she was going to sleep in her room or his.

"Can we talk?" she asked, her voice hardly more than a whisper.

The nerve in Neil's jaw worked. "If you come in and go anywhere near the bed, I might not let you leave until morning."

"Maybe I won't want to leave until morning."

"Are you saying—"

She blurted out, "I'm saying that I've never stood at a man's door like this before…that if you don't let me inside, you'll have to carry me somewhere."

Instead of stepping back so she could enter, he folded his arms around her and held her tight. "Knees still wobbly?"

She wrapped her arms around his neck. "Yes, but it doesn't matter. I know you'll catch me if I fall."

Then his smile faded. "I didn't want to force you into anything you didn't want…or that you'd regret."

"I'm here of my own free will. My only regret would be *not* coming to you tonight."

This time when Neil kissed her, he did sweep her away. He didn't hold back. He took as much as she could give and then he took some more. She couldn't distinguish his taste from hers and she didn't want to. She couldn't remember what it was like to take a breath and she didn't care.

Neil was hard against her. She could feel his heat through his shorts, through the thin layer of her gown. With him six inches taller than she was, neither of them could get the satisfaction they wanted. His hand slid down her back to her buttocks and lifted her. She wrapped her legs around him and

KAREN ROSE SMITH 151

her slippers fell off. He walked backward until they reached
the bed and then he sat with her, kissing her, until they tumbled
onto the mattress, each reaching for the other. They were as
hungry for each other as they had been the first time. Even
hungrier.

In spite of their eagerness, Neil didn't rush. He pushed the
spaghetti strap of her nightgown off one shoulder and tasted
her skin along her collarbone down to her breast. Her nightgown kept getting in the way so he helped her out of it, then
dropped his shorts.

After a long, teasingly seductive kiss, he whispered against
her lips, "Don't go away. I'll be right back."

She kept her eyes closed, still lost in desire. But she heard
him rifle through his duffel bag. In no time at all he was back.
Now she did open her eyes and what she saw in his took her
breath away.

"I want you so much my fingers are shaking," he admitted
wryly as he tore open the condom packet.

"And I want you so badly I'm shaking all over," she confessed. Taking the packet from him, slipping out the condom,
she waited for him to lie back so she could prepare him.

"Are you going to torture me?" he asked with a crooked
smile.

"I wouldn't call it torture." Her voice was as sensually
enticing as her fingers as they teased and tempted and then
finally rolled down the condom to cover him.

As soon as she finished, he pulled her to him for a kiss
and then rolled her over so he was on top. "This time I'm
not going to hurry."

"You hurried before?" she teased.

"I lost control before."

Then his mouth was on hers again and Neil filled her

senses and her mind and her heart. As he promised, he didn't
rush. He kissed every inch of her until she was mindless with
need, calling his name, begging for fulfillment. Finally he
entered her slowly, oh so slowly. When she lifted her hips to
take more of him, he chuckled, then continued his tempting
possession. By the time he filled her completely, she was
halfway there, rising fast, reaching for the farthest star. He
began thrusting, taking her farther and farther until she caught
the starburst and let it break all around her. His release
sounded just as satisfying, just as wrenching, just as heart-
enveloping. He said her name so tenderly tears burned in her
eyes. Moments later, he was cuddling her, holding her so
close she still felt one with him. She fell asleep that way,
dreaming of tomorrow.

Isobel had fallen asleep by the time Neil slipped away from
her and went into the bathroom. His mind was a turbulent maze,
his thoughts scattered and unfocused because of what had just
happened between them. She'd given herself to him completely.

So now what was he going to do? The phone call from his
supervisor, Derek Grayson, was a complication he'd never
expected. The mole, whoever it was, had digitally altered his
voice every time he called. Today he'd left a message on
Neil's supervisor's answering machine. Derek had repeated
it verbatim.

As Neil climbed into bed beside Isobel once more, he
studied her, knowing that this newest information certainly
wasn't true. The gist of it was that Isobel Suarez was taking
kickbacks from Pine Ridge Rehab.

How he wanted to tell her about it and trust her with the
information. But he couldn't. He had to go by the book. He
couldn't prejudice this investigation in any way.

Doesn't sleeping with her prejudice it? the devil's advocate inside his head asked.

No. Because he knew she wasn't guilty. He was absolutely certain.

He needed time to figure out what to do. But how much time could he give it? Could he get to the truth in the questioning he had left to do?

Or would he have to formulate a plan that could tear them apart?

Chapter Ten

The past week had been…

Neil couldn't even describe it as he lay beside Isobel in his room at the Inn after the senior center auction.

He ran his hand tenderly through Isobel's curly hair. She was cuddled naked by his side, nestled into his shoulder, and he wished he could keep her there forever. But after tomorrow, she'd look at him differently. He had hoped he wouldn't have to take the allegations against her to her supervisor. He'd hoped he'd have figured out over the past week who the mole was, that the information his office had received was groundless. But that hadn't happened and he had to get to the truth. His investigation had to take precedence over anything personal, didn't it?

Would Isobel ever forgive him for following regulations and keeping the charges against her to himself until they could be handled as *his* supervisor suggested? He hadn't needed Derek to remind him that if he gave the information to Isobel, she could clean up anything she'd been involved in. They had to go through the proper channels. As soon as he reported the claims against Isobel to her supervisor, he'd be on the phone to Pine Ridge, warning the administrators there not to talk to Isobel until the investigation was over.

"I can't believe we raised almost nine thousand dollars," Isobel mumbled against his chest.

"That's what you're thinking about at a time like this?" he teased, partitioning off his work from his personal life as he had all week. Each day they'd managed to steal time for themselves. This afternoon, they'd come back to the Inn, eager to undress and please each other in bed.

"What better time?" she returned. "I want to know why a bachelor needs a handmade quilt." There was a twinkle in her eyes as she sifted her fingers through his chest hair.

"My mother likes anything hand-crafted. It will make a wonderful birthday gift."

"You don't need it to keep you warm on long, cold nights in Boston?"

She was fishing and he knew why. What would happen to them once he was gone? Would he return to Walnut River? Would she come to see him in Boston? Would he date other women? He couldn't imagine ever dating anyone else. In fact, Isobel was the be-all and end-all of women for him. He found himself thinking about that house and picket fence and dreams he'd never imagined he could make come true.

Would she date other men? The thought of Isobel dating anyone else made his blood run cold.

"My condo has a great heating system." He had to keep this light. He couldn't get into anything deep, not tonight. All week he'd searched for ways to settle this investigation without using Isobel. But through his conference call with Derek yesterday, he'd realized there weren't any.

"Is something wrong? You're awfully quiet today."

"No, nothing's wrong. I'm just enjoying holding you like this. Besides, you wore me out yesterday, helping you get ready for the auction."

"I didn't wear you out. You were even running circles around Chad."

"He's a good kid. Did you know he's thinking about becoming a pharmacist?"

"Really? He told you that?"

"When we were carrying all those boxes to the storeroom in the senior center," he teased.

She lightly jabbed her elbow into his ribs.

Over the past week he'd learned her ticklish spots and he tickled her side. She squealed and wiggled away but he caught her and kissed her—longingly, sensually, almost desperately. When this was all over, how could he make her understand? How could he make her see that he was doing this for her, too? That if everything worked out, he'd clear her name and the hospital's, as well as find out who the informant was.

When he finished kissing her, he needed her all over again.

"I have to go soon," she murmured.

"Soon, but not now," he protested gruffly, caressing her face, running his thumb over her lips.

"I wish I could spend all night with you."

"You can."

"No, I can't. Dad would…he just wouldn't think it was right. And if anyone saw that I stayed over with you—" She shook her head. "I can't stay, Neil. I have to go home."

He knew she was right, yet he wanted another whole night, too. He wanted endless nights. That thought unsettled him, almost as much as the depth of his feelings for her. His emotions had been frozen for so long, he wasn't used to the happiness and the novelty of thinking about another person besides himself.

"Stay until dark," he coaxed, drawing her body on top of his, feeling her breasts against his chest, her softness against his hardness, her legs stretched out on his.

"So nobody sees me leave?" she asked.

"No, so we have at least another hour."

Isobel smiled at him. With her hands on his shoulders, she pushed herself up and straddled him. "Just what do you think can happen in another hour?"

"We can take each other to paradise."

Moving down lower on him, she let her hair brush his navel, then below his navel. He groaned.

"How about if you start the journey first," she suggested.

Then Neil couldn't speak as her lips surrounded him. He vowed when it was Isobel's turn, he had to make love to her as she'd never been made love to before.

If he did that, maybe when this was all over, she'd forgive him.

On Monday morning, at Northeastern HealthCare's main office in Boston, Anna Wilder adjusted her charcoal suit jacket and stepped up to the receptionist's desk in her boss's office suite.

Anna plastered on her professional smile. "Mr. Daly buzzed me this morning when I got in. He said he wanted to see me immediately." She shouldn't be nervous about this meeting but she was. She'd had only two other face-to-face meetings with Alfred Daly. One when he hired her, the other for a six-month evaluation. So why today?

His receptionist nodded. "Go on back. He's waiting for you."

The NHC building was plush. The company's logo was maroon and gray and the offices all kept that same theme, along with off-white leather furniture, contemporary artwork on the walls, and solid wood doors no one could hear through. That made her a little uneasy at times.

The door to Mr. Daly's office was open. When he saw her, he motioned her inside.

Daly was in his fifties, with brown hair combed over his bald spot. He wore suits that cost more than a month of her salary. And his ties? Some of his ties should hang in an art museum—many were one of a kind. When she saw him around the building, he never stopped to chat with anyone. He was always on the move, not unfriendly, just focused. Right now he focused on her.

"Anna, have a seat."

He stayed behind his monstrous mahogany desk, laid his reading glasses on the blotter and looked her straight in the eye. "I'll keep this short and to the point. I want you to go to Walnut River."

"Why?"

"There are many reasons, but mainly because you are a Wilder. Your sister and brothers are doctors at a hospital we want to bring into our family. Influential doctors. I know full well they're against the merger, and you've got to change their minds."

"I've talked to them many times. Their minds are set. I'm sorry, but there's nothing I can do about it."

"That kind of attitude won't get you far here, Anna. I want

you to make the merger between Northeastern HealthCare and Walnut River General happen."

"Even if I could convince my brothers and sister, there are many other doctors who are against it, as well as administrative personnel. How do you think I'm going to influence all those people?"

"That's my point, Anna. You have a job here for a reason. You're a smart woman. It's up to you to figure out how to accomplish the takeover. If you don't complete the merger, you will no longer have a job here."

Anna couldn't believe what she was hearing. Her whole professional career depended on this one assignment?

The truth was, for years she'd felt inferior to Ella and David and Peter. Now she had the chance to prove she wasn't. Now she had the chance to prove she could do what was asked of her and be successful in the hardest endeavor.

But what if she couldn't be? What if nothing she said or did made a difference?

Old insecurities die hard. She couldn't listen to them. "How soon do you want me to leave?"

"You and Holmes are working on the Carson Memorial Hospital merger. He tells me that's going well and you should have loose ends tied up in about a week. Is that right?"

"Yes, that's right."

"I don't want you to drop the ball there. I know you were instrumental in making it happen. So take this week to close that deal. But then I want you in Walnut River. I know you can do this, Anna. Don't let me down."

Anna stood. "I won't, sir."

As she left the office, she knew all she had to do was make the impossible happen.

If she thought about it too much, panic would overtake her.

For the next week, she'd concentrate on Carson Memorial. And then? She'd formulate a plan and go home to execute it.

Home. Where she didn't belong any more…where she'd never quite fit in.

And completing the NHC takeover would ensure she never did.

When Isobel returned to Walnut River General from an outside appointment early Monday afternoon, there was an e-mail from her supervisor, Mrs. Palmer, asking Isobel to come to her office as soon as she got back.

Margaret Palmer had hired Isobel and she'd always gotten along well with the woman. Margaret was in her late forties, knew that her social workers were overworked, and tried to be fair about assignments and their caseloads.

Isobel tucked her purse into the drawer of her desk and went down a short hall to Margaret's office. When she stepped inside, she was met by the most serious expression she'd ever seen on her supervisor's face. Margaret's ash-blond hair was styled in a pageboy, her bangs brushed to the side. Her glasses gave her a professorial look. Right now, Isobel saw confusion in her eyes and a frown on her face.

"You wanted to see me?"

Margaret motioned to the chair in front of her desk. Once Isobel was seated, her supervisor leaned forward and crossed her arms on her blotter. "I had a troubling report given to me this morning by Neil Kane."

A report from Neil? He hadn't said anything to Isobel about it. She remembered how quiet he'd been yesterday. Her heart began hammering. "What was in the report?"

"Mr. Kane has been made aware of a complaint against you."

"What?" Nothing could have surprised her more.

"A serious charge has been made against you, Isobel. Mr. Kane has received a complaint that you're taking kickbacks from Pine Ridge Rehab."

Isobel was so astonished, she couldn't form a coherent thought, let alone a coherent sentence.

"I have to take this seriously," Margaret went on, "especially since it's coming from an investigator from the Attorney General's Office. You're going to have to face the hospital review board and defend yourself." She hesitated. "Your review is set in two weeks. I'll have to suspend you until this is all cleared up."

"Suspend me? I haven't done anything wrong! All I've done is place patients the way I'm supposed to…in the best circumstances for *them.*"

As Margaret studied Isobel carefully, her expression became empathetic. "I know you're a hard worker, Isobel. I know you'll be able to clear this up."

Could someone be setting her up? Doing more than delivering rumors? "Is there any proof of this charge?"

"Mr. Kane didn't say if he has hard evidence or not. He'll be turning over whatever he has to the board."

"Don't I have a right to know what it is?"

"I suppose you can discuss that with Mr. Kane. You'll be receiving an official letter tomorrow. It will list the areas the review board will go over with you."

"I suppose my pay will be suspended, too."

"I'm sorry, Isobel, but yes it will be, until the review board makes a decision."

Isobel was still in a state of shock when she walked out of her supervisor's office fifteen minutes later after discussing who would work the cases under her supervision now. For the next half hour, she sorted her files and gave them to the case workers who would be attending to them. They shot her odd looks, and she wondered if they'd already heard about her review and suspension.

As she returned to her desk for her purse, she couldn't understand why Neil hadn't told her. Over the weeks he'd conducted his investigation, he'd come to believe the informant was giving him unfounded information. So why had he gone to her supervisor? Why was he pushing for a formal review? When she thought about the hours they'd spent together, the weekend they'd spent together, the emotional intimacy she'd never shared with anyone else, she felt betrayed and absolutely devastated. She was going to confront him to find out why he'd kept this from her, but she had to calm down. First, she'd visit her patients and tell them someone else would be handling their cases. She would assure them they were in good hands.

And then she'd go to Neil's office and confront him.

The fourth floor was quiet when Isobel approached Neil's office door. She was still shaken by what her supervisor had told her. The idea of confronting Neil hurt her heart. *Why* hadn't he told her?

Determined to learn the answer, determined to find out if she'd meant anything to him at all except a diversion while he was in Walnut River, she sharply knocked on the door.

With a cordless phone at his ear, he opened it.

She thought she glimpsed a flicker of…something in his eyes, but then it was gone. His expression showed not one iota of what he was thinking or feeling.

He motioned her inside while he crossed to the far end of the office to finish his call.

But she didn't sit. She unabashedly listened to his conversation as he said, "I have a few different options. I'll call you when it's over."

After he clicked off the phone, he laid it on the table beside his computer and focused his attention on her. "Did you speak to your supervisor?"

All of the hurt and sense of betrayal was pushing against Isobel. It wanted to come rushing out, but she held it off. She thrust it behind a dam of resolve. When she did, anger stole hurt's place. It fortified her and gave her the strength to meet Neil's gaze head-on. Her voice clipped and even, she demanded, "Why didn't you tell me there was a complaint against me?"

Still with no expression she could read, Neil suggested, "Calm down, Isobel. *Sit* down and we'll go through this."

"Don't patronize me, Neil. If you had to go before a review board, *you* wouldn't be calm, either. This could go to the state licensing board. Why didn't you tell me about the complaint?" she repeated. "And how long have you known about it?"

Neil turned the chair toward her. "Please," he said quietly.

She sat, not because he told her to, but because she was feeling shaky and didn't want to fall apart in front of him.

He lodged himself on the corner of the table, much too close to her. In spite of everything, she wanted to touch him, to feel his arms around her, to feel his skin pressed against hers.

Never again. Once trust was broken…

"I had to tell your supervisor first because this is my job. It's what I do. I have regulations to follow and I can't let anything interfere with those."

"How long?" She had to know if he'd been keeping this to himself while he'd made love to her. Had sex with her, she reminded herself. He couldn't love her and do this to her.

This was the first time since she'd entered Neil's office that he looked uncomfortable. "I learned about it last weekend. The call I received at my parents."

Her hurt won the battle to be released. "I thought we were…close."

"We were." His jaw set.

"No. If we were close, you never could have kept it from me while we…while we were in bed."

"I had to decide what to *do* about the information. I was hoping I'd find the mole and not even have to bring it to light. But by this weekend after talking with my supervisor— You've got to understand, I have to go by the book."

Hurt beyond words, she kept silent.

"Isobel, I'm doing this for a reason. I hoped you'd trust me."

"Trust you? I'd trust you if you'd told me about the complaint without going to Mrs. Palmer first."

"If I had told you, you could have tampered with possible evidence—spoken to contacts at Pine Ridge, wiped your hard drive of correspondence. With this review, our investigation of you is official."

Their eyes locked for a few seconds.

Neil's voice gentled. "I don't believe you're guilty."

That was something, she supposed, but not much. She understood about jobs and rules. To her, though, people came first. The people she loved came first.

Neil went on. "I want to use your stint in front of the review board to lure out the mole."

"How is ruining my professional reputation going to do that?"

"Obviously, you'll be able to answer every question and refute every charge. After you do, I'll announce that the allegations against you are groundless, just like every other charge I've investigated. I'm hoping the mole will get desperate and up the ante, give us more, let something slip."

"You're going to go public with my review?"

"I'd like your permission to do that."

She could see the merit in his idea. If the mole had a grudge…or if he was getting paid to aid NHC in the takeover, he wouldn't stop. He'd want to stay in the fight and damage the hospital even more thoroughly. But Neil was using her career and her reputation as the means to his end.

"In other words, you want to use me as a pawn."

He contradicted her. "You need to look at this differently. You'll be my partner, not a pawn."

"You're *using* me, Neil. Don't delude yourself that you aren't. I understand why. You're stumped. You don't know where else to go. Walnut River General can't fight this takeover attempt until you're gone. Because of that, for the sake of the hospital, I'll help you with this. I'll do what you want. But on a personal level, I don't want any more to do with you."

She heard him call her name as she ran out of his office, as she kept running down the hall to the back stairway and took each step faster than she should have. Neil didn't come after her and she wasn't surprised. He didn't care about her after all—he cared about his investigation. He saw her as an easy way to make the days in Walnut River go faster. She'd been the foolish one to fall head over heels in love with a man who saw her as a means to an end.

She could lose her job. Oh, maybe that wasn't what he had in mind. Maybe that wasn't what he'd intended. But anything could happen with something like this, especially if someone was trying to set her up to prove wrongdoing at Walnut River General. Why couldn't Neil see that? Why couldn't he see that if he'd come to her with the complaint, they could have figured out together what to do with it?

Now, she was suspended. Her dreams were yesterday's news and Neil's so-called ethics had betrayed her.

A small voice inside her challenged her. *He's just doing his job.*

If doing her job meant hurting someone she cared about, she wouldn't be able to do it. It was as simple as that. Black and white.

Neil looked at life in black and white, too. Obviously, rules and regulations came first with him.

At the bottom of the stairwell, she pushed open the outside door and stepped into the warmth of the May day. But she didn't feel the warmth. She was cold inside. She needed to clear her head so she could start functioning again.

Her life would go on without Neil Kane in it. End of discussion.

When she reached Sycamore Street, she parked two houses down from her dad's. She didn't want him to know she was home. Some nights she was much later than this so he wouldn't worry. Thank goodness she kept a duffel bag in the car with a change of clothes.

After changing into workout clothes in the garage, she tied her running shoes and tried not to think. More importantly she tried not to feel. She knew there were tears on her cheeks and hoped the wind would dry them.

Wheeling her bike out of the side door, she bumped it over the grass until she had it on the gravel alley. Then she hopped on and took off as if she were in the most important race of her life. She didn't even think about where she was headed. She just rode, down neighborhood treelined streets, pedaling hard up the hills, letting the wind and speed take her as far as it would. She barely noticed when she veered off the side streets onto the secondary road.

When she came to an intersection, she turned right, aware cars were passing her and that her bike lane was very narrow. But the cars zooming by didn't distract her because she was so intent on not feeling, not thinking, not caring. Through all the "nots," however, she couldn't blank out the image of Neil's face. She couldn't forget how the gold flecks in his eyes were more prominent after he kissed her or how his hair dipped over his brow when they tussled in bed. Most of all, she couldn't eliminate from the tapes playing in her head the sound of his gentle voice saying, *I don't believe you're guilty.* He'd been sure of her honesty. Yet he still wanted to use her? And if he'd use her in this…

Had she ever really been his lover? Or had she been just a plaything? Tim hadn't cared enough about family. She'd thought Neil was different. He'd interacted with her dad and her nephew so well. Had that all been an act, too?

"What is real?" she shouted to the trees and the sky and anyone who cared to hear.

As she looked up to heaven, praying for an answer, she missed seeing the pothole until it was right in front of her. Maybe on a normal day, she could have navigated it. But today—

She hit the edge of the pothole, skidded on the loose chunks of asphalt, banged into the weather-worn crater and tumbled onto the lower shoulder of the road, hitting her head hard on the edge of the concrete.

Chapter Eleven

Isobel regained consciousness in the ambulance and panicked when she saw the IV, felt the oxygen at her nose, and realized she couldn't move. Her neck was held into place by a brace and she was lying on a body board.

Paramedic Mike O'Rourke, Simone's fiancé, patted her arm. "It's okay, Isobel. We're going to take care of you. We have you strapped down pretty tight just to make sure nothing moves until we can get some tests at the hospital."

Her face felt raw and burned like crazy. Her head hurt, too. A lot. And her ankle ached more than she wanted to think about. "I…I hit a pothole, didn't I?"

"That's what a witness at the scene said. He pulled over and called 911 on his cell phone." Mike pumped up the blood-pressure cuff on her arm. "What were you trying to do? Win the Tour de France?"

The memory of her disastrous meeting with Neil came rushing back. Tears swam in her eyes.

"Hey now," Mike said as he grabbed a tissue and dabbed at a tear on her cheek. "I told you, you're going to be fine."

The other attendant adjusted the IV line. "ETA two minutes."

Isobel had to admit she didn't like being on the receiving end of care at Walnut River General. She had no control and she hated that.

A few minutes later, Simone was by her side when the gurney was wheeled into the emergency room. She looked worried. "What did you *do?*"

"I rode my bike too fast," Isobel said, trying to joke.

"Do you want me to call your family?"

"Can you call Debbie? But tell her not to call Dad until I have whatever tests the doc is planning. I don't want Dad to worry. I don't even have my insurance card. It's in my purse in the garage. Debbie might have to tell him what happened if she picks that up."

"All right, Isobel," Simone soothed, looking worried. "Stop trying to plan everything. Let's just get you taken care of."

Mike wheeled her gurney into an E.R. cubicle and there the examination and questions began.

Three hours later, Isobel felt as if she'd been poked and prodded and examined and tested to the limit. Her father, Debbie and Chad stood around the gurney in the emergency-room cubicle looking at her with concern and worry. "I'm fine," she told them again. "I just have to wait for the doctor's final orders, then I can go home."

"You have a concussion," Chad reminded her.

"Only a slight one."

"Thank goodness you were wearing your helmet," her father mumbled, "or you could have cracked your skull wide open. I don't know how you're going to climb the stairs with that ankle all wrapped up like that."

"That's why it's wrapped, Dad, so I can put some weight on it."

Debbie muttered, "You should have let me call Neil."

"No!" Isobel said with a firmness that told her sister not to bring it up again.

Chad turned away from the bed, stepped toward the door to look out into the hall and check his watch. Isobel knew he was probably concerned about his brother and sister. A neighbor had come over to stay with them.

To her relief, the doctor hurried into the small room, studying her chart. He was tall and thin, probably in his late forties. Dr. Ruskin was fairly new on the staff, so Isobel hadn't had many dealings with him. But she knew Simone liked him.

"You're going to hurt tomorrow," he said, shaking his head. "Put ice on your ankle as needed for the next twenty-four hours. After that, warm baths will help. I have a prescription here for anti-inflammatory medication. I'd rather you not take anything for pain for twenty-four hours. You've had a concussion and I don't want medication masking that. You'll need someone with you for the next day or so. Through the night, I want someone to awaken you every three to four hours to make sure you're alert, conscious and have all your faculties."

"Is that really necessary?" Isobel wanted to know. "I just have a headache."

"It's necessary, Miss Suarez, and I can't let you go until I know someone's going to do that for you."

"I'll stay with her tonight and check on her every few hours," a deep male voice said from the doorway.

To Isobel's surprise and dismay, Neil stood there in jeans and a black T-shirt. His hair was wet as if he'd just taken a shower.

"What are *you* doing here?" Isobel asked with as much heat as she could muster. He was the last person she wanted to see. She didn't know when she'd felt quite this bad and she was sure she looked worse than she felt. She had scrapes on her cheek and probably a bruise was beginning to show. The doctor had put a dressing on it and she was supposed to change it in the morning. Her hair still had gravel in it from her brush with the side of the road and the scrapes down one arm had also been bandaged. Her ankle, which had twisted on the pedal when she'd fallen, was throbbing almost as much as her head. On top of all of that, she was wearing a very flimsy hospital gown that had seen way too many washings.

Isobel turned accusing eyes on Debbie.

"Don't look at me," her sister said, holding up her hands in surrender.

"I called him," Chad admitted, stepping up to the side of the bed. "I thought he'd want to know."

She could have groaned. She hadn't told anyone what had happened between her and Neil. She'd just insisted that she didn't want Debbie or her dad to call him. But Chad, who thought he knew best—

Neil came over to stand beside Chad and clapped the boy on the shoulder. "He was right to call me, Isobel. Your dad can't drive and you know he has trouble with the stairs. He also needs his sleep. I can run up and down and stay awake all night. I'll only stay as long as necessary, tonight and tomorrow, then you can kick me out."

Both her father and Debbie were looking from Neil to her and back again as if trying to figure out what was going on. She couldn't explain it now. She wasn't about to explain it now. Maybe not ever. Just why Neil was doing this, she didn't know.

But then he murmured in a low voice near her ear, "I feel responsible for what's happened. And you know your dad's not up to par yet. You don't need to burden him with your care right now."

"What happened is my *own* fault," she whispered back. "I ran into a pothole."

"Right. Would you have done that if you weren't so upset?"

Taking a glance over Neil's shoulder, she saw her sister and dad were trying to overhear. All of a sudden she felt such fatigue she couldn't fight them all anymore.

"All right," she said loud enough for the doctor to hear.

Neil straightened. "Is there anything else I should know before I take her home?"

"The nurse will give you a list of instructions when she brings the wheelchair."

"Wheelchair?" Isobel and Neil exclaimed at the same time.

The doctor gave Isobel a sly smile. "You work here, Miss Suarez. You know it's standard procedure, even for you."

Debbie slipped over to Isobel's side. "I brought you a clean pair of sweats. I'll help you get dressed."

"We'll be in the waiting room," Neil said as he and her dad stepped into the hall.

Though the doctor followed them out, Chad lingered behind. "Did you and Neil have a fight or something?"

"Or something," Isobel mumbled. Then seeing Chad's glum expression, Isobel gave him a small smile. "It's okay.

I know you did what you thought was best. Dad won't worry about me so much if Neil's there."

She could handle this, she told herself. She could. She'd just pretend Neil was a stranger checking on her now and then. In many respects, he was.

"Maybe you and Neil can work out whatever's wrong while he's there," Chad suggested.

Chad was too young to realize what a rare commodity trust was. She felt so betrayed by Neil she could never trust him again—not trust him to put her first, not trust him to feel what she did for him, not trust him to stay rather than go. She and Neil wouldn't be working on any differences. Not tonight.

Not ever.

Awkward didn't begin to cover the way Isobel felt as Neil hovered over her after her dad opened the door.

Taking Isobel's elbow, he helped her up the step into the house. Although his touch wasn't meant to be personal, even almost clinical, it *was* personal. She could remember every way and every time he'd touched her.

"They should have given you a cane," he remarked gruffly.

As she hobbled to the foot of the stairs, just wanting to make it to her own room and shut the door, she said over her shoulder, "I'm fine. Really."

Her father announced loudly, "I'm going to watch the History Channel for a while. If you need me, you holler."

She turned toward her dad, trying to ignore Neil's tall presence beside her. "Thanks for coming to the hospital."

"You know I'd do anything for you, Iz," her father returned.

Her eyes misted over and she grabbed onto the banister to lever herself up to the first step.

"If you think I'm going to stand here and watch you try to hobble up each one of those stairs, you're mistaken."

The next thing she knew, Neil had swept her into his arms and was carrying her up the staircase. She was too surprised to protest. Even if she had protested, by the look on Neil's face, she knew it wouldn't have done any good.

At the top of the stairs he asked curtly, "Which way?"

She pointed toward the door to her room.

Carrying her inside, he gently set her down on the bed. Only the glow of the hall lamp shone into the room and she couldn't see his expression. Before he slipped his arms away from her, she thought she felt him hesitate. But then he was standing beside the bed, turning on the lamp, looking down at her as if he were mad at the world.

"This wasn't your fault, Neil, and I'm not your responsibility. So why don't you just go back to the Inn?"

"Your dad's worried sick about you. He'd be climbing up and down these stairs, not getting any sleep, checking on you every hour. Is that what you want?"

"Of course that's not what I want!"

"Then stop fighting me. At least on this. You didn't have any supper tonight. What can I get you?"

"I really just want to wash up and go to bed."

"You need to take your anti-inflammatory pill first and it has to be taken with food. So what's it going to be?"

If she weren't hurting so much, if she weren't so exhausted, she might laugh. Somebody taking care of her was indeed a novelty. *She* was the caretaker and she didn't like this reversed role.

Surrendering, she suggested, "A piece of toast and a glass of apple juice."

"Coming right up." Soberly he left her room.

As soon as Neil closed the door behind him, Isobel moved. When she did, her head pounded, but she ignored it. After she grabbed her nightgown and robe from her closet, she hurried out into the hall to the bathroom. She did as best as she could in the amount of time she had, washing away any remaining grime with her washcloth, using her honeysuckle soap to do it. A few minutes later, she was crossing the hall to her room again, holding on to the door frame for support when Neil came up behind her.

"Are you feeling light-headed?"

He carried her toast on a dish with a vial of pills, the juice in his other hand.

"A little. I have an awful headache. I'll be fine once I can close my eyes and turn out the lights."

Once she'd settled in bed again without his help, this time under the sheet, he watched her eat and take her pills.

He ran his hand gently over the gauze on the side of her face. "Does this hurt?"

If she told him it didn't, he'd know she was lying. "I think it's going to look worse than it feels," she joked. Then she added, "I hope I have some gauze patches in the linen closet. I need to change this in the morning."

"I'll check before I go downstairs. I'm only going down to keep your dad company for a few minutes, though. I'll be sleeping in the spare bedroom. I'll set my alarm and check on you every few hours. If you need anything—*anything,* Isobel—you call me. In fact, do you have your cell phone?"

"It's in my purse." She pointed to the other side of the bed.

Neil didn't ask her permission but rather went around the bed, fished in her hobo bag, and found it. Opening it, he said, "I'm going to put my cell number on your speed dial. I'm sure I'll hear you if you call me, but if I don't, use this." Coming around the bed again, he set it on the edge of her nightstand.

He was looking at her as if he wanted…wanted to…kiss her? No, couldn't be, and she certainly didn't want to kiss him. So she concentrated on the pounding in her head, the soreness on her cheek, the thump of her ankle.

Pulling the sheet up to her chin, she said, "Good night, Neil."

She didn't thank him because she couldn't. She didn't want him here. Just looking at him made her hurt even more. Her heart felt as if it had a hole in it and that was worse than any bicycle fall, any concussion, any physical injury.

As if he understood that, he nodded. "I'll check on you in a little while."

When Neil left the room, she let the dressing on her cheek catch her tears. Then she turned onto the side of her face that didn't hurt, eager to escape her life for sleep.

Neil lay on the spare-room bed in John Suarez's house, staring at the ceiling. There was an almost-full moon tonight and the shadows played around the room. He concentrated on their lines and edges, trying to stop his mind from clicking through recriminations that were too many to count.

Isobel's accident was *his* fault. Everything about this messed-up situation was his fault. The best thing he could do for Isobel was stay away from her. She'd never forgive him for putting rules and regulations before her. For the first time in his life, he was questioning the way he lived it.

The alarm on his watch beeped. Immediately he swung his legs over the side of the bed, willed his thoughts and reactions into neutral and headed for Isobel's room. There he stood at her bed, watching her sleep in the moonlight. She was curled up on her side, facing away from him, her hand tucked under her uninjured cheek. As John had said repeatedly, thank goodness she'd been wearing a helmet.

Isobel's curly hair was a mussed tangle. It lay on her pillow and he longed to stroke his fingers through it, catch them in the curls and feel their silkiness once more. She'd only used the sheet to cover herself. He could see the outline of her beautiful body underneath it and his gut tightened. How could he even be thinking—

As if she sensed him watching her, she uncurled her legs and turned over onto her back. "Neil?" Her voice was soft and feathery, filled with drowsiness. The fact that she recognized him was a good sign.

He hunkered down by the side of the bed. He could ask the usual questions—what's your name, where do you live, who's the President of the United States—but he opted for, "How do you feel?"

"Like a truck ran over me. A very big truck."

"Do you know where you are?"

"In my old room in my dad's house."

He hated to bring it up, but a reality check was a reality check. "Do you know what happened to you?"

She hesitated a moment, gazing straight into his eyes. He could almost hear her thinking, *Neil Kane happened to me.* However, she answered, "I was riding my bike on the highway and hit a pothole in the bike lane."

She'd given him details so he'd know she remembered all of it. She was alert, even while sleepy, and he was relieved.

"Are you dizzy?"

She shook her head and winced. "No, but I feel a whole

lot better if I don't move my head. Was Dad all right when
he went to bed?"

Even in her condition, hurting all over, she worried about
the people she cared about. He was no longer in that circle.
And the idea that he wasn't gave him a feeling of loss he'd
never experienced before. "I reassured him that you just need
a few days and you'll be feeling a lot better."

As they stared at each other in the shadowy room, Neil
couldn't look away. So many emotions bombarded him, his
chest tightened.

Before he could stop himself, he reached out and cupped
Isobel's uninjured cheek in his palm, his thumb tracing her
nose and the curve of her upper lip. "I wish I could take all
the hurt away." He wasn't just talking about her bike accident.

She lay perfectly still, then she moved away from his hand
and whispered, "You'd better go."

Moving away from her was so difficult…but necessary.

Standing, he jammed his hands into his pockets. "I'll be
back in a couple of hours. I'll leave after I make you and your
dad breakfast."

She closed her eyes and he knew why—so she didn't have
to look at him and remember how he'd reported her to her
supervisor…so she could block him out of her life.

Feeling numb inside, he turned and left her room. Numb
was better than feeling too much.

In the morning, Isobel knew she looked worse than she had
the night before. The bruising had set in and the adrenaline
that had rushed through her after the accident had ceased. She
absolutely didn't want to get out of bed. More because she
didn't want to face Neil than anything else.

Even her suspension.

What was going to happen to her professional reputation? Would she always have a questionable cloud hanging over her head from the review?

Frustrated, she hiked herself up, took a deep breath, and swiveled until her feet were on the floor. If she couldn't keep her job in the social work field, she'd find *something* else. Even if she had to wait tables until she figured out what to do.

Fifteen minutes later, she'd dressed and was stepping into a pair of deck shoes when there was a knock on the door. "Isobel, are you up?"

If she didn't answer, would Neil go away? Didn't she *want* him to go away?

"I'm up," she called.

He came in and saw immediately she was dressed in a pale-green T-shirt and matching knit shorts. "I thought you might need help going downstairs."

She wished he'd waited to come up, or not felt as if he had to help her at all. "I have to change my dressings and retape my ankle."

"I'll help you. It's hard doing that for yourself."

She could protest from here to next year and he wouldn't listen. She already knew that about Neil. When he found a direction, he took it.

After Neil took the gauze pads from the linen closet, she sat on the bed. He used antiseptic on her face, fumbling once. Did he just feel awkward or…?

Was his heart racing, too? Did he feel as unsteady as she did?

She wasn't even sure if she meant anything to him… anything more than a responsibility.

She hardly took a breath. He must have showered this

morning because he smelled like the bathroom soap. He hadn't shaved, though. The beard stubble gave him a rough, sexy look.

As if he could *look* any sexier…

They avoided each other's gazes until the gauze pad slipped again and she caught it. His hand covered hers and for an interminable second, neither of them moved or breathed.

When he took the gauze from her hand, he assured her, "I'll be finished in a minute."

And he was.

Why couldn't she stop wanting him? Why couldn't she stop feeling as if she needed him? He certainly didn't need her. She was expendable, a blip in his investigation that he could use to find out what he wanted.

In spite of all that, she couldn't forget the dream that she'd found her Mr. Right. Yet he wasn't right. He was all wrong for her. Wasn't he? Hadn't he betrayed her? In spite of that deep sense of betrayal, his body seemed to pull hers toward him. She could hardly keep from leaning in… couldn't stop wishing he was touching her in a much different way.

When he finished gently taping her ankle—his long fingers on her leg and foot much too tempting, much too personal, much too intimate—she felt wrung out.

After her murmured thanks, Neil set her foot on the floor. "If you're worried about being reported to the state licensing board, you shouldn't be. I know the complaint against you has no legs. There weren't any witnesses to back up the charges."

"Unless someone is setting me up. What if somebody really wants to harm me?"

Neil adamantly shook his head. "This is about NHC, not about you."

"I hope so," she said in a low voice, turning away. She couldn't look at him and not remember what she thought they'd been to each other. Apparently he couldn't look at *her*, either.

Closing the box with the gauze pads, he suggested, "It would be a lot easier if I carried you downstairs."

"No!" There was no way she was going to let him hold her in his arms again. No way at all. "I have to do it on my own so I know I can. I'll use the banister. I'll be fine."

"Just because you keep saying that doesn't make it so. Come on. I'll go down the steps ahead of you so you don't fall."

She'd already fallen. That was the problem. She'd tumbled head over heels in love with Neil. But she'd get over it. She'd get over him.

She had no choice.

A few minutes later, after Neil watched her hobble to the stairs, he went down sideways, watching her as she held on to the banister and maneuvered down each step.

"You *are* going to stay downstairs for the day, aren't you?" he asked with a frown.

"What I do isn't any of your concern anymore."

At her words, his frown deepened to a scowl, but he didn't argue with her, just studied her like the proverbial hawk until she was on the first floor.

Her father, in the kitchen reading the morning newspaper, smiled at her. "How are you doing this morning?"

"Much better."

"Liar," Neil whispered into her ear so close she could feel his breath on her neck. Her chin went up.

"I'm not dizzy anymore and the headache's better. I'll be

able to go back to work—" She stopped. She couldn't go back to work even if she did feel better.

The expression on her face must have given something away because her dad asked, "Isobel?"

"We'll talk about work later, Dad." She glanced over at the man who had unsettled her life. "After Neil leaves."

As Neil ignored the dig and took a frying pan from the cupboard, her father's gaze swung from one of them to the other. "All right, tell me what's going on."

"Not now," Isobel insisted as she made her way to the table and sat in one of the chairs.

"Yes, now," her father demanded. "I want to know why Neil feels he has to take care of the two of us, and why you're treating him like a stranger."

The silence stretched, becoming a heavy weight in the kitchen until Neil broke it. "My office received a complaint about Isobel. I reported it to her supervisor."

Isobel's dad studied her expression. "It sounds as if Neil was caught between his job and you. Is that why you're so upset?"

"I'm upset because he didn't tell me about it. Because he didn't give me a chance to explain or figure out what was wrong before he blew my career to bits."

"There are channels and regulations," Neil protested, cracking an egg savagely.

"And there was *us*," Isobel maintained, her voice shaking.

"I think you two have a lot of talking to do." Her dad pushed himself up from his chair.

"There's nothing to talk about. I'll be lucky if I still have a job when this is done," she blurted out, close to tears. "I'm suspended, Dad, until everything is cleared up. When I feel better, I'll look for something to hold us over."

"You're acting like a martyr," Neil grumbled. "The hospital review is less than two weeks away."

"If this were *your* job on the line, you wouldn't be so glib," she tossed back as her father slipped out of the kitchen to give them privacy. But she didn't want privacy, didn't even want to be in the same room as Neil. Everything would be different if he had just told her. If he'd told her, they could be getting to the bottom of it together. If he'd told her, she wouldn't feel so alone. If he'd told her, she would have known they really were lovers, not only in bed, but in life.

Close to tears again, she managed to say, "I'd like you to leave now. Dad and I can handle breakfast on our own."

"Isobel—"

"Please go."

He must have heard the finality in her voice, because he didn't glance back at her as he left the kitchen.

A few minutes later she heard the front door close. She dropped her head into her hands and cried.

Chapter Twelve

Ever since her meeting with her supervisor—and her confrontation with Neil—Isobel had vacillated between anger and hurt.

She hadn't spoken to him since he'd left her dad's house last Monday. Did he know if the hospital had turned up any concrete evidence against her? Even if he did, he wouldn't tell her. He went by the book, she thought bitterly.

Unable to do her job, she was going to visit Florence MacGregor—unofficially. After all, they'd become friends and she wanted to know how the older lady was doing. There was no chance of running into West on a Monday afternoon. He'd be working. Maybe her visit would make Florence's day a little brighter, and would, in turn, brighten hers. It was worth a try.

Pine Ridge Rehab was located on the west side of town, surrounded by lawns and, of course, pine trees. The one-floor facility was sprawling and accommodated about fifty residents at any one time.

Since Isobel didn't know if the staff had heard about the accusations against her, she decided to avoid the main lobby and reception area. She entered through a side door and stepped into a hall south of the dining room. Since it was almost three, Florence should be back in her room resting.

Isobel heard applause from the game show channel as she stopped at the door to Florence's room and peered inside. The older woman was seated in an armchair, her walker beside her. She pointed to one of the contestants on *The Match Game*. "I told you the answer was pink. It's *pink* elephant."

Isobel smiled, rapped softly on the door and stepped inside.

"Isobel!" Florence exclaimed. "I haven't seen you for—" She stopped as if she couldn't remember. "For a very long time."

Isobel's ankle was healed now and she just had a few remnants of the scrape on her cheek that she'd managed to cover with makeup. "I've been a little under the weather. I had an accident on my bike."

Florence examined Isobel's face. "West told me that you weren't at work. That you had a concussion. Do you still have headaches?"

Isobel could see this was one of Florence's more alert days. "Not anymore." She pointed to Florence's walker. "How are you doing? You should be able to go home soon."

"Tomorrow or the next day," Florence assured her. "That's what West said. But I don't know how long I'm going to be at home. West tells me I'm going to take a trip."

"To Las Vegas?" Isobel wouldn't be surprised if West took his mother there to have some fun after she'd recovered.

"No, not Las Vegas. Let me see. Where did he say we were going?"

Maybe Florence just imagined she was going on a trip. "It doesn't matter. Wherever you go, I'm sure you'll enjoy yourself."

"He told me the leaves would be magnificent in October. That's when we're going. October."

All of New England was beautiful in October. Then again, maybe Florence was confusing this October with last October. Isobel recalled West had taken some vacation time last fall, too. "Has West mentioned where you'll be staying when you go away? What hotel?"

Florence looked absolutely blank for a moment. "He told me but I can't remember. Why can't I remember, Isobel?"

She leaned closer to pat Florence's hand. "It's not important. I'm sure he picked out a very nice hotel." Since his mother liked to gamble, maybe he was taking her to Foxwoods Resort in Connecticut. But Isobel didn't want Florence to get more upset or frustrated when she couldn't find what she was looking for in her memory.

"Lily came to see me again," Florence told Isobel.

"She did? That's terrific. It's good to have visitors. It makes the time go faster."

"She came when I didn't have therapy. She stayed a long time."

Isobel guessed Florence's friend had come on Sunday afternoon. "She brought me candy," Florence announced like a little kid who had received a Christmas present she liked. "Chocolate-covered creams. They're in that box over there if you want one."

Isobel spotted the box on the bedside table. "Would you like one?" she asked Florence, guessing that might be why she brought it up.

"Sure."

Isobel rose and went to the nightstand. Bringing the box back to Florence, she lifted the lid and the wonderful smells of chocolate and mint floated up.

Florence pointed to the square ones. "Those are mint. They're my favorite."

"What are the round ones?"

"They're coconut or vanilla."

Isobel reached for one of those, though she wasn't hungry. She hadn't had any appetite since last week. But maybe the sugar would give her some of the energy she was lacking. And sharing the treat with Florence formed a bond.

Florence took a mint one and poked it into her mouth. She smiled as she enjoyed the candy. "Do you like to cook, Isobel?"

"I do when I have the time."

"A young lady here was talking to West about when I go home. She told him I should have someone stay with me and cook for me."

Isobel had wondered what Florence's caseworker here at the rehab facility would recommend to West.

"He said he found someone—a college girl who's living at home for the summer. She's going to spend her days with me."

"She'll be nice company for you."

"I guess. Do you think she'll like to watch the game show channel?"

"I don't know. You'll have to ask her when you meet her."

"She'll have to go back to college, though. That's why West is taking me to Fair Meadows when we go on our trip." Florence snapped her fingers. "That's the name of the place I'll be staying. Fair Meadows."

Isobel went still. Everyone in health care in Massachusetts knew about Fair Meadows, outside of Boston. It was one of the elite nursing-care facilities for patients with Alzheimer's. Politicians sent relatives there, and so did movie stars. How could West afford the place?

Not exactly sure where to go with this, but knowing she had to go somewhere, Isobel commented, "I think you'll like Fair Meadows very much. I've heard the grounds are beautiful with lots of gardens. There's a sunroom. They even have someone on staff who'll give massages."

"They have a hair salon, too," Florence interjected.

How would West's mother know that? Unless she'd seen a brochure, or maybe a promotional DVD. "I guess West told you all about it."

"I saw it. I went to that hospital in Boston and then he took me to Fair Meadows. He wanted to see if I would like it."

Isobel's suspicions grew. "Do you remember when you went?"

"Not so long ago. It was…let me think…it was before Christmas." She thought some more. "Before Thanksgiving."

Apparently West had taken his mom to Boston last fall for a medical evaluation. Why wouldn't he have told the staff here? Why wouldn't he have mentioned it to Dr. Wilder?

Isobel was getting a very bad feeling about this. "Tell me something, Florence. I know West works very hard to take care of you. He puts in a lot of hours at the hospital. But I was just wondering, does he have another job, too?"

"How did you know?"

Maybe this wasn't what Isobel thought. Maybe West actually was working two jobs in order to pay for Fair Meadows. But even with two jobs…

"Does he do work at home at night for someone else?" She felt terrible pumping Florence, but if her suspicions were true, she had to know what else West was doing.

"He gets papers at home sometimes. You know, that machine he has beeps. And he's on his computer a lot."

"It could be work from the hospital that he's taking home."

"No, I don't think so. Because I found an envelope with money in his desk from somebody else. Not Walnut River General."

"Were there any papers with the money? A pay stub?"

"Let me think. The money was new. I could tell. There wasn't a paper with it. But on the envelope up at the top in the corner there was a little picture of one of those things a doctor wears."

Isobel's heart thumped harder. "A stethoscope?"

"Yes, that's it. A stethoscope."

"And beside the stethoscope were there letters? NHC maybe?"

"Oh, I don't remember the letters, but I do remember the stethoscope."

That was good enough for Isobel. NHC's gray-and-maroon logo with initials and a stethoscope was well-known by now. West MacGregor was the mole who was siphoning information to Neil's office.

Chad's basketball ran around the rim and then dropped into the basket. "I'm three up on you," he crowed. "You said you wanted to play but I think your mind is somewhere else."

Neil caught the ball as it bounced on the asphalt. Yeah, his mind was somewhere else all right. When Chad had called him after school, asking if he wanted to play after he got off work, Neil had agreed. He needed the exercise. He needed to expend some energy. He needed to stop thinking about Isobel.

When Neil dribbled the ball, Chad dashed in front of him

to guard him. "Aunt Iz was over here yesterday. She wasn't limping. She said her head didn't hurt anymore. But…"

Neil stopped dribbling. "But?"

Snatching the ball from him, Chad made another shot. "See what I mean? Distracted. Because of her, I'll bet. She didn't seem very happy, either."

"I guess not," Neil muttered.

"I heard her telling my mom you got her suspended and she might even lose her license."

"That's *not* going to happen." He'd been tempted to go to Pine Ridge and question the staff himself. But the hospital's lawyer was doing that. And Neil couldn't interfere. The phrase *by the book* rang in his ears again.

"Neil?" Chad asked him.

"What?"

"Aren't you and Aunt Iz even talking?"

"No."

"How are you going to get back together if you're not even talking?"

Back together. Had they *been* together? He thought about the weekend in Cranshaw. He thought of the week afterward. Of how many times they'd made love. The ways they'd made love. The conversations after they'd made love. He'd talked about his childhood and so had she. They'd talked about their college years. They'd kissed and connected and—he'd known all that time he'd have to report Isobel to her supervisor.

By the book. His job didn't give him the satisfaction it used to and he'd hated keeping something from Isobel.

"What's the problem, Neil?" Chad asked, standing still now.

"My job's the problem." Then he thought about *that* statement. "Nix that. *I'm* the problem. For so many years I've lived by rules and regulations that they've become second nature to me. I put my job and what I'm doing here ahead of Isobel's feelings."

After a thoughtful silence, Chad asked, "Remember when you asked me if my wanting a car was more important than Stephanie?"

"I remember."

"Is your job more important than Aunt Iz? If it is, then what she thinks and feels doesn't matter. But if it isn't, if *she's* more important—"

Chad had decidedly turned the tables on him. Neil thought about not caring about Isobel, what she thought and felt. He considered not seeing her again. Not kissing her again. Not holding her again. A video played in his mind of the last couple of years, of his work, of his life, of his practically empty apartment, of the days on the road and the nights in motels. The work had been important. But now, being here in Walnut River, this job, this investigation, seemed to be all smoke and mirrors. He'd let it come first out of habit, not out of a great deal of thought. Whenever he pictured himself going back to Boston without Isobel, not seeing her for weeks on end, now maybe not seeing her ever, he knew that wasn't right for his life. He knew—

That he loved her.

How could he have thought that this affair with her was just about sex? How had he ever thought that betraying her wouldn't push them apart?

Deep down, had he wanted to push them apart? Did he feel that unworthy of being loved?

The question was immense and couldn't be answered easily. Couldn't be answered here and now.

Chasing the ball that had rolled down the driveway, he

scooped it up and dribbled it back to the net. "Game on," he said to Chad. "I bet I can recover those points."

The beep-beep-beep from his cell phone, which was lying with his keys and his wallet and duffel bag near the porch, stalled the game once more. As he jogged to retrieve it he called to Chad, "We'll get this going again in a minute." He opened the phone and saw Isobel's number. His heart began racing. Did she want to talk to him? Was it possible she could forgive him?

"Isobel?"

"Neil, I need to talk to you. I've been driving around and around, trying to decide what to do."

"What happened?"

She hesitated.

"Isobel, you can trust me."

"No. No, I can't."

His heart ached when she said those words, but he knew they were true. She didn't think she *could* trust him. Coaxing wouldn't make her open up to him. But *she* had called *him,* so he waited, hoping.

"I have to see you. I might have information that could end your investigation."

The constriction in his chest loosened a little because she wanted to see him. "I'm at your sister's, playing basketball with Chad. Do you want to come over here?"

Silence echoed back and forth for a few moments.

"I don't want to get Debbie involved in this. The Crab Shack is closed today. How about if I meet you there?"

"You want to make sure you're not seen with me."

"You don't want to be seen with me, Neil. Remember? Your investigation comes first. I'm putting it first. I'll see you there in ten minutes."

He took the phone from his ear, stared at her number and then closed it. She'd told *him*. And there hadn't been a hint of forgiveness in her tone. Maybe betrayal didn't deserve forgiveness. But he was glad she had called him. And whatever she had found out, he'd use it to clear her, to get this job over and done with and then to get on with his life.

Right now, he just wasn't sure whether Isobel would be in it or not.

Fifteen minutes later, Neil waited for Isobel at the same table where they'd shared a basket of crabs after he'd first arrived in Walnut River. As he watched her park and climb out of her car, he knew she was remembering, too. Her eyes were bright with unshed tears and her expression was sad.

Wearing jeans and a red knit top, she approached him slowly. He could tell she'd lost weight. From the bike riding regimen she had started? Or because, like him, she had no appetite anymore?

It was the last week in May. Birds twittered in the trees and the long, green grass swayed in the wind. Yellow and blue irises bloomed in clumps along the path to The Crab Shack, while tiny yellow flowers blossomed in the field. He wished, oh, how he wished, he was meeting Isobel here for a romantic rendezvous.

Stopping a few feet from him, she glanced over her shoulder as if she were afraid someone was following her. "I know who your mole is. It's West MacGregor."

The accountant. Neil remembered the man who had been cooperative, but not too cooperative—who had defended Walnut River, but who had asked questions of his own. "How do you know?"

"I went to visit his mother at Pine Ridge." If Isobel

expected a comment from him, she didn't get it. If she wanted to visit her former patients, that was her business—at Pine Ridge or anywhere else.

"I heard from one of the aides I interviewed that she has dementia?"

Without commenting on that, Isobel explained, "Today Florence was alert and quite talkative. I thought West took her on a vacation last fall. That was the story they both told. But today I learned he took her to Boston, probably to be evaluated for Alzheimer's. He also showed her around an upscale nursing facility for Alzheimer's patients. And I do mean upscale. It's nothing he could afford on *his* salary. When Florence told me about it and I questioned her more, it seems West is being paid by Northeastern HealthCare. Their logo is a stethoscope with their initials. Florence described it as being on an envelope with cash she found in West's desk."

Neil considered everything Isobel had told him. "He could deny all of this. It's his word against his mother's."

"You mean this information isn't useful?" Isobel looked crestfallen. She'd thought she had discovered the answer to the problems at Walnut River and he'd just told her she hadn't.

He reached out and grabbed her arm. "We can use this, Isobel."

When she pulled away from him, their gazes met, and he saw the distrust in hers. "I'll make something work. I want your name cleared as much as you do."

His words obviously surprised her. "I doubt that."

"I will do *anything* to clear your name. I got you into this mess. If I hadn't pushed so hard, if I had stayed away from you, no one would have seen you as a threat."

She seemed to consider that. "What are you going to do?"

"I'll have to convince someone to feed information to West MacGregor—information he can use against the hospital. If he calls it into my supervisor's office again, then we'll know he's the mole."

She stood very still and studied him carefully. "I'll do it."

"No. I don't want you any more involved in this than you are."

"We don't want him to get suspicious."

"You're suspended. You don't have the opportunity to tell him anything."

"I'll make the opportunity to drop off some papers to Margaret that I filled out for the review. I know when West takes his break. He does it like clockwork. I'll pretend I'm looking for Simone in the lounge."

"And what if someone else walks in?"

"I'll make it work, Neil. I don't know why you're having a problem with this. You were ready to use me as a pawn before the review board."

He couldn't deny her accusation and her blow struck hard. If he told her now he'd made a mistake—

Anything personal between them had to wait until this was all over. He didn't want her to feel used again. He didn't want to make her promises he couldn't keep. He had to make a few decisions on his own before he could tell her what she meant to him. He had to be ready for action...because words wouldn't mean anything now. Not to Isobel.

"Are you sure you want to do this? A few of the personnel I interviewed this week want to get to the bottom of this as much as I do. I think they'd be cooperative and could feed information to West."

"I know West. He'll believe me. And he has to believe what we tell him."

"Do you know what you'll say?"

"I'll keep it simple. I can be righteously indignant about the whole proceeding, proclaim my innocence, then tell him I know specific instances where patients were charged for medicine they never received."

"Were they?"

"No. But West doesn't have to know that."

"He might want specifics."

"I'll give him specifics. I'll give him fake names."

"He could check." Neil knew he was playing devil's advocate, but he wanted this to work.

"Yes, he could. But I doubt if he will. Sure, everything's computerized. But you saw what it was like trying to go through the files. Sometimes you can find what you're looking for and sometimes you can't. Do you know how many patients go through our hospital in a year? He'd never expect *me* to lie to him."

"What if Florence tells him you were there asking questions?"

"I didn't really ask questions. I just guided her. He won't think it's unusual that I stopped in if she even remembers to mention it. If we do this right away, we should have our best shot."

"I admire your courage in doing this." He wanted to kiss her, give her a hug, show her how much he *did* care.

"It's not courage. It's fear and desperation."

"You'll tell him tomorrow?"

"Tomorrow." She checked her watch. "Dad will be worried about me. I need to go home." She turned to walk away.

"Isobel?"

Although she stopped, she didn't turn around. Maybe because she guessed he had something personal to say.

"When this is all over, you and I need to talk."

If she heard him, she didn't acknowledge that she did. She went to her car, climbed in and drove away.

Neil was so tempted to go after her. Even if he did, she still wouldn't trust him. Even if he did, she still might not forgive him.

He had to prove to her he cared about her. And he would, when this was all over.

When this was all over.

Chapter Thirteen

"I don't like this," Neil said for at least the fifth time, as his fingers accidently brushed the undercup of Isobel's bra.

In the garage to the rear of her dad's property, he finished fastening a piece of tape on the wire that Isobel would be wearing during her conversation with West MacGregor. The warrant that he'd picked up from the district attorney was stuffed into his inside jacket pocket. The Walnut River chief of police, Rod Duffy, would be meeting him at the hospital in plain clothes.

Isobel didn't flinch at his almost intimate touch. But she didn't look at him, either. This was probably more difficult for her than for him. After all, he wanted to be touching her. She didn't want *him* anywhere near *her*.

"West is the mole," Isobel protested. "If I can get him to admit it and you have it on tape, you can close your investigation."

The information Isobel had fed West yesterday had been called into Neil's supervisor. West was obviously desperate, using anything he could get hold of. But they needed the proof that he was the man behind the digitally altered voice.

"I don't want you to push him." Neil finished with the adhesive tape and adjusted the wire. Afterward he took Isobel by the shoulders. "If you can't get anything out of him, you leave. Owen Randall, the chief of police and I will be two offices away. That one was empty and we won't arouse anyone's suspicions by being there."

Isobel buttoned the blouse that complemented her skirt and reached for her jacket. "You'll be able to hear everything?"

"Everything."

Neil stooped to the ground to toss the tape into the duffel bag he'd used to carry the equipment. He glanced over at Isobel.

Staring at the bag, her voice was soft and shaky when she asked, "I don't really know you at all, do I?"

They had to be at the hospital in fifteen minutes and couldn't talk about this now. "You *do* know me, Isobel. This is just another part of my job. White-collar crime is still crime."

She finished buttoning her jacket, felt for the small microphone and asked, "Can you see anything?"

Her face reddened when he took an extra few seconds to assess her appearance. "You look normal. I can't tell a thing. Give me a five minute head start. After I park at the back entrance, I'll come up the stairs. And don't worry. I'll be in place before you get to West's office."

"How will I know for sure?"

"You're going to have to trust me, Isobel."

Neil could feel her eyes on his back as he left, hoping their plan worked…hoping even more fervently Isobel would place her trust in him again.

* * *

Isobel shook as she stood outside West's office, praying Neil was ensconced in the empty one down the hall. Sure, she was nervous about confronting West. But she couldn't forget the feel of Neil's fingers on her skin as he'd arranged the wire and then taped it. She'd tried to pretend he was a stranger, just doing his job, but the look in his eyes said he wasn't. The look in his eyes said that he had regrets, too.

Attempting to shake off her feelings about Neil, she focused on what she had to do. West's door was partially open. She poked her head inside. "Can I talk to you?"

The accountant looked surprised to see her but then he pasted on a genial smile. "Isobel. Did you have another meeting with Margaret?"

Why else would she be here? After all, she was suspended. And that was *his* fault. "No. I came to see you." Inside his office now, she closed the door. "You've been outed, West."

Was that fear she saw in his hazel eyes? "I don't know what you mean. Explain yourself, Isobel." Her colleague wasn't smiling now.

"I told you about overcharges in drugs to Mrs. Johnson and Mr. Talbot."

West was wary. "So you did."

"That information was called into the State Attorney General's office. Neil Kane knows about it."

West tried to play the conversation with nonchalance. "Are you and Mr. Kane speaking again? Rumor has it there was a rift between you two."

"It's over, West. I told Neil there *were* no charges. I just gave you that information to see if you were the mole. And you are." She wanted to make this sound as if it were *her* idea…that she intended to trap him to save herself.

Shaking his head in denial, anxiously balling one hand into a fist, he said, "They can't prove anything, Isobel. It's my word against yours. I can claim *you* called in the information. After all, with a device to disguise your voice—"

Isobel cut in. "How do you know the mole disguised his voice? There's only one way. You made those calls, West."

Sweat broke out on his brow and he appeared almost desperate. Then he sat up straighter. "As I said, you can't prove it. No one can. It's not as if I even did anything illegal. I called in rumors—rumors that deserved to be investigated. They were based on facts."

"Why? Why did you do this? You put the reputation of the doctors here in jeopardy, the reputation of the hospital itself."

Now some of the panic left his face and he appeared almost defiant. "Why? Oh, Isobel, grow up. There's only one why. NHC is paying me. I need the money for Mom's care. She deserves the best and I'm going to give it to her. She's not going to end up a ward of the state. I know what those nursing facilities are like. No one cares there. I need to have her someplace where I don't have to worry about her twenty-four hours a day. You know what that's like. We've talked about it. What would you have done if this was your father?"

What *would* she have done? Sold his house and everything he owned so she could pay a year or two of good care?

"I don't know what I would have done, West. But not this. I wouldn't have affected other lives."

"Don't be so righteous. You're on the outside looking in. When you're on the inside, you get a different picture. Black doesn't stay black and white doesn't stay white. They merge into gray."

She could see how that had happened for West.

He was frowning now. "I never intended things to go this

far. NHC approached me. They knew I had taken Mom to Boston for an evaluation. They knew her prognosis wasn't good. They said if I helped them with the takeover they would make sure she had a place at Fair Meadows, and I wouldn't have to worry about her care."

"That's what you're getting out of this?" Isobel asked, feeling sorry for him in spite of herself.

"They gave me money to cover her needs for home care until I'm ready to put her in Fair Meadows. How could I refuse that, Isobel? How?"

He had asked her what she would have done. And the answer had seemed so simple, so easy. But now looking at it from his perspective, wanting the best for his mother, life definitely *wasn't* black and white.

The door to West's office opened and Neil burst in. Behind him she caught a glimpse of Owen Randall and the chief of police.

West stood and stuttered. "What's this? Why are you here?"

Isobel said sadly, "I'm wearing a wire, West. They've recorded everything you said." Then she added, "I'm sorry." Because she was. She and West had been friends of sorts. She hated deception of any kind. And she'd just deceived him. For the greater good.

For the greater good. Is that what Neil had done to her? She glanced up at him. "Do you need me here?"

His voice was gentle. "Just leave the equipment in the office down the hall. I have to tie up loose ends here."

He motioned West back into his chair. "Have a seat, Mr. MacGregor. I have a ton of questions and we'll be here all night if we have to be."

"I want to sit in," Owen interjected forcefully.

"You can if you wish, but I don't think there's any need,"

Neil concluded. "My findings aren't official yet, of course, but as far as *I'm* concerned this investigation is over."

Rod Duffy extended his hand to Isobel. As she shook it, he said, "You did good work here today."

Owen nodded in agreement and added, "As soon as we verify that MacGregor's information was false, I'll notify Margaret. We'll be canceling your review. Why don't you take the rest of the week off and start back on Monday?"

Start back on Monday. As if everything was going to go back to normal. As if none of this had even happened. She suspected Northeastern HealthCare would deny they'd requested West MacGregor's help. They still wanted to take over Walnut River General and that endeavor wouldn't stop just because Neil had uncovered West's role in it.

When she moved to pass Neil, he clasped her arm. "I admire your courage."

Admiration? Did he feel anything else?

Today had been enlightening in so many ways. One point that had been driven home was that the situation hadn't been black or white for Neil, either. Would he call her later? Did she want him to?

She was so confused she just didn't know.

Although West had been silent since Neil's entrance, he said now, "I'm not going to answer any of your questions. I want a lawyer."

"You can call a lawyer. But if you tell me what you know, I can put in a good word for you with my boss." Neil reminded him, "We have you on tape and Isobel is a witness."

West rubbed his forehead wearily. Finally he nodded. "All right."

Neil gave Isobel one last look before she left West's office, and she couldn't decipher its meaning.

She needed time to think, time to put everything into perspective.

And if Neil didn't call?

She'd go on as she had before, working and taking care of her dad.

Isobel couldn't have been happier for Simone and Mike. The blue sky, puffy white clouds and golden sun had been a perfect backdrop for their ceremony in the rose garden of Mike's parents' backyard. Now Isobel, along with Mike's huge family, Simone's mom, Ella Wilder and her fiancé J. D. Sumner tossed birdseed along with good wishes at the bride and groom as they ran around the side of the house to Mike's SUV, climbed inside and drove away, waving back through the words *Just Married* written in soap on the rear window.

Isobel and the other guests smiled at each other as the couple drove away.

Mike's brother motioned to all of them. "Come on. There's a lot of party left in that backyard. My mother doesn't want leftovers for the next week."

As everyone laughed, Isobel trailed behind Ella Wilder as she and J.D. settled at one of the linen-covered tables under the canopy. Mike's mother cut second pieces of cake for all. Isobel sat staring at hers, not in the least bit hungry. It had been a beautiful late-afternoon ceremony, but her heart had felt like a rock in her chest as she'd witnessed the happy couple share their vows, exchange rings and dance their wedding dance.

The past two days she'd had time to think about Neil and everything that had happened. Had he been torn by what he'd had to do? Had turning the information over to her supervisor been difficult for him? *Had* she been more than a diversion while he was in Walnut River?

He hadn't called her before he'd left. From what she'd heard, he'd left the same day West had confessed. That hurt, too. Granted, she hadn't given him reason to think—

Ella, who was planning a wedding with J.D. for the fall, turned toward Isobel. "I just love your dress."

Isobel had found a calf-length, multicolored, flowered dress with a sweetheart neckline and a pencil-slim skirt at one of Walnut River's boutiques. "Simone insisted I buy something I could wear again."

"It's perfect for a wedding or anything dressy in the summer. I love the style. Maybe my bridesmaids could find something like it in fall colors."

There were weddings all around Isobel. Peter and Bethany's next month, Ella and J.D.'s, Courtney Albright and David Wilder's the weekend before Thanksgiving.

"Are you getting excited?" Isobel asked Ella, knowing the answer already from the sparkle in her eyes.

"I started writing my vows," Ella admitted. "J.D. said it's the perfectionist in me. I want them to be perfect."

J.D. draped his arm around Ella's shoulders and gave her a hug. "I told her I'm just going to stand up there and say what I feel. But she thinks I should write down the words so I don't forget."

Suddenly, Ella and J.D. were staring over Isobel's shoulder.

Isobel glanced behind her—and was astonished to see Neil Kane. He was wearing a suit and tie and was too handsome for words. Her heart skipped a beat, then ran so fast she could hardly catch her breath. Why was he here?

Finding her voice, she managed to say, "I—I thought you'd left."

His gaze focused on her as if she were the only guest at the reception. "I did. I had a lot to accomplish in two days, but I managed it, and that's why I'm here." He held out his hand to her. "Will you come talk with me?" He nodded to the patio and the glider there.

Isobel didn't know what to say or what to do or how to act. But she knew if she didn't take Neil's hand, she'd forever have regrets. When she put her hand in his, his fingers enveloped hers. She stood, her mouth bone-dry, and followed him to the patio, away from the crowd of guests. She knew everyone was watching them. But Neil didn't seem to be bothered by that.

When he motioned to the glider, she sank down onto it and he lowered himself beside her, still holding her hand. It was as if he didn't want to break the connection, however tenuous it might be.

"I was wrong." His deep voice was strong, sure and apologetic.

Now she definitely couldn't breathe.

"I was wrong to put my job before *you*. Doing that made you think I didn't care about you, that I just wanted to use you to get to the bottom of the investigation. That wasn't true, Isobel. I've done a lot of soul-searching since the day I turned the information over to your supervisor. Ever since I met you, you rocked my world. The night we spent together in Cranshaw— I'd never had a night that intense with a woman before. The following week I told myself we could continue the affair long-distance. I thought I could control my emotions about you, that I could set them apart from the investigation. But I couldn't. Remember what your father said? That I worked the way I did because I didn't want to be close to my ex-wife?"

Isobel nodded.

"I realized that, yes, I was doing my job the 'right' way by going to your supervisor. But by doing that I was also pushing you away, even though what I wanted most was to be close to you. I told you I felt responsible when Garrett died, whether my feelings were rational or not. I think all these years I've believed I didn't deserve love because I didn't love him enough. I was pushing you away because I didn't deserve you…didn't deserve to be loved by you."

"Oh, Neil."

He squeezed her hand. "Let me finish. I guess I've come to realize the best way to serve Garrett's memory is to love *more,* not less. To accept love whether I deserve it or not. I love you, Isobel. I don't want an affair with you, I want to spend my life with you. I know I've hurt you, and I have to do more than say the right words. So…the past two days, I've been rearranging my life. I've resigned my position at the Attorney General's Office, effective in two weeks."

"You're not serious!"

"Yes, I am. I'm going to get my private investigator's license and do investigative work for the D.A.'s office in Pittsfield."

"Pittsfield?" It was actually dawning on her that Neil had arranged his life around hers.

"Yes, Pittsfield. It's only a half-hour commute. I'll probably still have odd hours. This isn't nine-to-five work. But we can live in Walnut River. We can buy a house or build a house with an apartment for your dad."

"You want my dad to live with us?"

Neil smiled at her words. "Yes. Remember? He and I get along really well." His smile faded away as he asked, "Can you forgive me? Can you believe that from this day on I'll put you first?"

Gazing into his eyes, seeing truth and love there, her reply came from her heart. "Yes, I can forgive you. I've been doing a lot of thinking, too. I've realized that just because you followed the rules didn't mean you didn't care about me. You were caught in the middle. I guess I…was still insecure… afraid my feelings were one-sided. I should have tried to understand."

Instead of kissing her, which is what Isobel wanted Neil to do, he stood. Before she could grasp what was happening, he went down on one knee before her, holding a beautiful marquise-shaped diamond ring between his fingers. "Up until now I've handled everything all wrong. Now I intend to handle it right. I want to start my life with you today. Will you marry me, Isobel? Will you accept this ring as a promise that I will join my life with yours and make you as happy as I possibly can?"

She was overcome by the love and the hope in Neil's eyes. Tears welled up in hers as she easily found the answer to all of her confusion and all of her questions. "I love you, too, Neil. Yes! Yes, I'll marry you."

After he slipped the ring on her finger he stood, pulled her to her feet and wrapped his arms around her. His kiss told her everything that was in his heart. It was a promise that their future lay before them and that they would walk into it together.

Their hunger for each other was intense and demanding. Isobel received Neil's passion and gave her own until—

The sound of applause finally penetrated the haze of desire, love and need surrounding them. Neil broke away, and still holding her, murmured close to her ear, "I think we have an audience."

They both turned their attention toward the guests gathered

under the canopy. The clapping grew louder until, with one arm still around her, Neil held up a hand.

Grinning, he declared, "She said yes."

There were cheers and calls of congratulation. And then Neil was kissing her again, lifting her into his arms and carrying her away from the rest of the guests.

"I didn't give up my room at the Inn. How about if we go there for a while and then tell your dad the good news?" he proposed.

"A while?" she teased.

"Why don't you call your dad on the way? Tell him I'll bring you home after we've made wedding plans."

"Is that what we'll be doing?" she asked innocently.

"Yes. In between showing each other the perfect married couple we're going to be."

"Perfect," she agreed, knowing she *had* found her Mr. Right.

She held on to him as he carried her to his car and he held on to her, ready to start the journey of promises, commitment and love that would last a lifetime.

* * * * *

THOROUGHBRED LEGACY
*The stakes are high when it comes to love,
horse racing, family secrets
and broken promises.*

*A new exciting Harlequin continuity series coming soon!
Led by* New York Times *bestselling author
Elizabeth Bevarly*
FLIRTING WITH TROUBLE

Here's a preview!

THE DOOR CLOSED behind them, throwing them into darkness and leaving them utterly alone. And the next thing Daniel knew, he heard himself saying, "Marnie, I'm sorry about the way things turned out in Del Mar."

She said nothing at first, only strode across the room and stared out the window beside him. Although he couldn't see her well in the darkness—he still hadn't switched on a light…but then, neither had she—he imagined her expression was a little preoccupied, a little anxious, a little confused.

Finally, very softly, she said, "Are you?"

He nodded, then, worried she wouldn't be able to see the gesture, added, "Yeah. I am. I should have said goodbye to you."

"Yes, you should have."

Actually, he thought, there were a lot of things he should have done in Del Mar. He'd had *a lot* riding on the Pacific

Classic, and even more on his entry, Little Joe, but after meeting Marnie, the Pacific Classic had been the last thing on Daniel's mind. His loss at Del Mar had pretty much ended his career before it had even begun, and he'd had to start all over again, rebuilding from nothing.

He simply had not then and did not now have room in his life for a woman as potent as Marnie Roberts. He was a horseman first and foremost. From the time he was a schoolboy, he'd known what he wanted to do with his life—be the best possible trainer he could be.

He had to make sure Marnie understood—and he understood, too—why things had ended the way they had eight years ago. He just wished he could find the words to do that. Hell, he wished he could find the *thoughts* to do that.

"You made me forget things, Marnie, things that I really needed to remember. And that scared the hell out of me. Little Joe should have won the Classic. He was by far the best horse entered in that race. But I didn't give him the attention he needed and deserved that week, because all I could think about was you. Hell, when I woke up that morning all I wanted to do was lie there and look at you, and then wake you up and make love to you again. If I hadn't left when I did—the way I did—I might still be lying there in that bed with you, thinking about nothing else."

"And would that be so terrible?" she asked.

"Of course not," he told her. "But that wasn't why I was in Del Mar," he repeated. "I was in Del Mar to win a race. That was my job. And my work was the most important thing to me."

She said nothing for a moment, only studied his face in the darkness as if looking for the answer to a very important question. Finally she asked, "And what's the most important thing to you now, Daniel?"

Wasn't the answer to that obvious? "My work," he answered automatically.

She nodded slowly. "Of course," she said softly. "That is, after all, what you do best."

Her comment, too, puzzled him. She made it sound as if being good at what he did was a bad thing.

She bit her lip thoughtfully, her eyes fixed on his, glimmering in the scant moonlight that was filtering through the window. And damned if Daniel didn't find himself wanting to pull her into his arms and kiss her. But as much as it might have felt as if no time had passed since Del Mar, there were eight years between now and then. And eight years was a long time in the best of circumstances. For Daniel and Marnie, it was virtually a lifetime.

So Daniel turned and started for the door, then halted. He couldn't just walk away and leave things as they were, unsettled. He'd done that eight years ago and regretted it.

"It *was* good to see you again, Marnie," he said softly. And since he was being honest, he added, "I hope we see each other again."

She didn't say anything in response, only stood silhouetted against the window with her arms wrapped around her in a way that made him wonder whether she was doing it because she was cold, or if she just needed something—someone—to hold on to. In either case, Daniel understood. There was an emptiness clinging to him that he suspected would be there for a long time.

* * * * *

THOROUGHBRED LEGACY
coming soon wherever books are sold!

Thoroughbred Legacy

Launching in June 2008

A dramatic new 12-book continuity that embodies the American Dream.

Meet the Prestons, owners of Quest Stables, a successful horse-racing and breeding empire. But the lives, loves and reputations of this hardworking family are put at risk when a breeding scandal unfolds.

Flirting with Trouble

by *New York Times* bestselling author

ELIZABETH BEVARLY

Eight years ago, publicist Marnie Roberts spent seven days of bliss with Australian horse trainer Daniel Whittleson. But just as quickly, he disappeared. Now Marnie is heading to Australia to finally confront the man she's never been able to forget.

The stakes are high when it comes to love, horse racing, family secrets and broken promises.

A new exciting Harlequin continuity series coming soon!

Cole's Red-Hot Pursuit

Cole Westmoreland is a man who gets what he
wants. And he wants independent and sultry
Patrina Forman! She resists him—until a Montana
blizzard traps them together. For three delicious
nights, Cole indulges Patrina with his brand of
seduction. When the sun comes out, Cole and
Patrina are left to wonder—will this be the end of
the passion that storms between them?

Look for

COLE'S RED-HOT PURSUIT

by USA TODAY bestselling author

BRENDA JACKSON

Available in June 2008 wherever you buy books.

Always Powerful, Passionate and Provocative.

Romantic
SUSPENSE

Sparked by Danger, Fueled by Passion.

Seduction Summer:
Seduction in the sand...and a killer on the beach.

Silhouette Romantic Suspense invites you to the hottest summer yet with three connected stories from some of our steamiest storytellers! Get ready for...

Killer Temptation
by **Nina Bruhns;**
a millionaire this tempting is worth a little danger.

Killer Passion
by **Sheri WhiteFeather;**
an FBI profiler's forbidden passion incites a
killer's rage,

and

Killer Affair
by **Cindy Dees;**
this affair with a mystery man is to die for.

Look for

KILLER TEMPTATION by Nina Bruhns in June 2008
KILLER PASSION by Sheri WhiteFeather in July 2008
and
KILLER AFFAIR by Cindy Dees in August 2008.

Available wherever you buy books!

Visit Silhouette Books at www.eHarlequin.com   SRS27586

Royal Seductions

Michelle Celmer delivers a powerful miniseries in
Royal Seductions; where two brothers fight for the
crown and discover love. In *The King's Convenient Bride,*
the king discovers his marriage of convenience to the
woman he's been promised to wed is turning all too
real. The playboy prince proposes a mock engagement
to defuse rumors circulating about him and restore
order to the kingdom…until his pretend fiancée
becomes pregnant in *The Illegitimate Prince's Baby.*

Look for

THE KING'S CONVENIENT BRIDE
&
THE ILLEGITIMATE PRINCE'S BABY

BY MICHELLE CELMER

Available in June 2008 wherever you buy books.

Always Powerful, Passionate and Provocative.

REQUEST YOUR FREE BOOKS!
2 FREE NOVELS PLUS 2 FREE GIFTS!

SPECIAL EDITION®
Life, Love and Family!

YES! Please send me 2 FREE Silhouette Speâal Edition® novels and my 2 FREE gifts (gifts are worth about $10). After receiving them, if I don't wish to receive any more books, I can return the shipping statement marked "cancel." If I don't cancel, I will receive 6 brand-new novels every month and be billed just $4.24 per book in the U.S. or $4.99 per book in Canada, plus 25¢ shipping and handling per book and applicable taxes, if any*. That's a savings of at least 15% off the cover price! I understand that accepting the 2 free books and gifts places me under no obligation to buy anything. I can always return a shipment and cancel at any time. Even if I never buy another book from Silhouette, the two free books and gifts are mine to keep forever.

235 SDN EEYU   335 SDN EEY6

Name   (PLEASE PRINT)

Address   Apt. #

City   State/Prov.   Zip/Postal Code

Signature (if under 18, a parent or guardian must sign)

Mail to the **Silhouette Reader Service:**
IN U.S.A.: P.O. Box 1867, Buffalo, NY 14240-1867
IN CANADA: P.O. Box 609, Fort Erie, Ontario L2A 5X3

Not valid to current subscribers of Silhouette Speâal Edition books.

Want to try two free books from another line?
Call 1-800-873-8635 or visit www.morefreebooks.com.

* Terms and prices subject to change without notice. N.Y. residents add applicable sales tax. Canadian residents will be charged applicable provinâal taxes and GST. This offer is limited to one order per household. All orders subject to approval. Credit or debit balances in a customer's account(s) may be offset by any other outstanding balance owed by or to the customer. Please allow 4 to 6 weeks for delivery. Offer available while quantities last.

Your Privacy: Silhouette is committed to protecting your privacy. Our Privacy Policy is available online at www.eHarlequin.com or upon request from the Reader Service. From time to time we make our lists of customers available to reputable third parties who may have a product or service of interest to you. If you would prefer we not share your name and address, please check here. ☐

SSE08

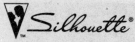

COMING NEXT MONTH

#1903 A MERGER...OR MARRIAGE?—RaeAnne Thayne
The Wilder Family
For Anna Wilder, it was double jeopardy—not only was she back in
Walnut River to negotiate a hospital takeover her family opposed,
the attorney she was up against was long-ago love interest Richard
Green. Would the still-tempting single dad deem Anna a turncoat
beneath contempt...or would their merger talks lead to marriage
vows?

#1904 WHEN A HERO COMES ALONG—Teresa Southwick
Men of Mercy Medical
When nurse Kate Carpenter met helicopter pilot Joe Morgan in the
E.R., their affair was short but very sweet...and it had consequences
that lasted a lifetime. Kate had no illusions that Joe would help raise
their son, especially when he hit a rough patch during an overseas
deployment. Then her hero came along and surprised her.

#1905 THE MAN NEXT DOOR—Gina Wilkins
Legal assistant Dani Madison had learned her lesson about men the
hard way. Or so she thought. Because her irresistible new neighbor,
FBI agent Teague Carson, was about to show her that playing it safe
would only take her so far....

#1906 THE SECOND-CHANCE GROOM—Crystal Green
The Suds Club
When the fire went out of his marriage, firefighter Travis Webb
had to rescue the one-of-a-kind bond he had with his wife,
Mei Chang Webb, and their daughter, Isobel, before it was too late.
Renewing their vows in a very special ceremony seemed like a good
first step in his race for a second chance.

#1907 IN LOVE WITH THE BRONC RIDER—Judy Duarte
The Texas Homecoming
Laid up after a car crash had taken all that was dear to him, rodeo
cowboy Matt Clayton was understandably surly. But maid-with-a-
past Tori McKenzie wasn't having it, and took every opportunity to
get the bronc rider back in the saddle...and falling for Tori in a big
way!

#1908 THE DADDY PLAN—Karen Rose Smith
Dads in Progress
It was a big gamble for Corrie Edwards to ask her boss, veterinarian
Sam Barclay, if he'd be the sperm donor so she could have a baby.
But never in her wildest dreams would she expect skeptical Sam's
next move—throwing his heart in the bargain....

SSECNM0508

SPECIAL EDITION